68 Kill

Bryan Smith

First Print Edition
Copyright 2013, Bryan Smith
All Rights Reserved
www.bryansmith.info

Cover design copyright 2013 by Kristopher Rufty
http://lastkristontheleft.blogspot.com/

Formatting by Denise Brown
www.maydecemberpublications.com

All rights reserved. No part of this publication may be reproduced or transmitted in any form or by any means without the permission of the author. All the characters in this book are fictitious, and any resemblance to actual persons, living or dead, is coincidental.

This one is for Kent Gowran.

1

This wasn't about the money. At least it wasn't only about the money. It was more about what the money represented. Freedom. Liberation. A chance to catch a damn breath, an opportunity to get out from under that mountain of overdue bills and finally pay off all that back rent. He wouldn't be doing something like this otherwise, because he just wasn't the kind of guy who did things like what he was about to do.

These were the things Chip Taylor told himself as he sat there in the shotgun seat of Liza's Pontiac Grand Prix with a loaded 9mm pistol clutched in his gloved right hand.

These things were rationalizations.

Justifications.

On an objective level, he was totally aware of that. But he needed to tell himself these things. If he didn't, he wouldn't be able to play his role in Liza's crazy scheme. He wasn't a bad guy. A villain. He had always seen himself as a decent person. Good-hearted and law-abiding. The kind of guy who always did the right thing in any situation. This meant he had to fool himself into believing what he was about to do was a necessary evil. It was a total Robin Hood kind of deal, when you got right down to it. They were going to take from the rich and give to the poor. Only it wasn't truly as altruistic as that, what with the two of them being the "poor" part of the equation. It wasn't like they were gonna drop the money off at a church or give it to some needy fucking orphans.

Liza shot him a steely look. "You ready for this?"

"Yeah."

"You sure?"

Chip scowled. "Of course I'm sure. Why do you keep asking me that?"

"Because you seem really nervous. Your hands are shaking."

Shit.

She was right. The hand gripping the gun was trembling. He willed the tremors to stop as he stared at the 9mm. It was the real deal. An instrument of death. The bullets inside it were real. They could make holes in people. *Kill* people. Liza had scored the guns from a street dealer. She had guns of her own, legally purchased ones, but those were for home protection only. *These* guns had been purchased specifically because there was no legal record of the transaction. They could not be traced back to either of them in the event something went wrong. Looking at the gun, Chip felt keenly aware of how easily something *could* go wrong.

This was a potentially deadly escapade they were about to embark upon. There was no getting around that unsettling truth. But it should be easy. The way Liza had explained it, they should be able to get in and out in just a few minutes. There were just two people in the house. Middle-aged, out-of-shape people. They were wealthy and could afford to lose a single fat stack of cash. They had no reason to resist them or take any kind of unnecessary risk.

Not for a mere sixty-eight thousand dollars.

Chip released the breath he had been holding and looked Liza in the eye. "I'm okay. I'm ready."

Liza's expression didn't change, but she nodded. "Good."

She pulled on a black ski mask and Chip did the same.

They got out of the car.

2

The car was parked at the curb on the opposite side of the street from the target house. Cars lined the curb on both sides of the street. It was right around the time most families in this neighborhood would be going to bed, which meant very few people were out and about. The neighborhood was an old one, but it was located adjacent to a trendy area. The houses here were nice—especially in light of their age—but they weren't mansions. If they worked quickly and with efficiency, they could do this thing and get away without being noticed.

Liza quickly crossed the street and started across the lawn toward the side of the house. Despite his assurances to the contrary, Chip remained a bundle of nerves. The porch light was on and there were dim lights on inside the house. Lamps, probably. The porch light was likely on to provide an extra level of half-assed security. Half the porches on this block were similarly lit up. Lamps suggested some obvious things—people reading while lying in bed or sitting in a living room recliner. So he heaved a huge sigh of relief once he had safely joined Liza in the shadows at the side of the house. He had felt naked and exposed running across the lawn. It had taken mere seconds, but had seemed so much longer than that.

Liza glanced back at him as they moved past a buzzing HVAC unit and approached the six-foot-high wooden fence that encircled the small back yard. "Give me that flashlight."

The little flashlight was stowed in an inner pocket of his jacket. He took it out and gave it to Liza, who had been here several times and knew exactly where she needed to go.

Liza switched it on and aimed the beam at the fence, illuminating a gate. A metal padlock of impressive size was hanging open on a hasp. Chip had known to expect this, but the actual sight of it made him shake his head. It stunned him to learn how careless—how stupid—people with so much money could be. They were almost begging to be robbed.

Liza slid the lock out of the hasp and tossed it over her shoulder. It landed with a muted thunk on the ground.

She reached for the gate handle.

Chip put a hand on her shoulder. "Hold on."

Though he couldn't see her face due to the ski mask, he could envision her expression by the narrowing of her eyes and the harsh twist of her lips. The mixture of impatience and contempt came through loud and clear. "Jesus, Chip. The sooner we get this over with, the better. It's too late to turn back now."

Actually, that wasn't true it all. Not yet. They hadn't done anything so far, other than trespass. They could go back to the car and drive away, just go on with their regular, dreary, debt-laden lives as if they had never entertained committing several serious felonies. For a

fleeting moment, he thought about saying just that. It would be the smart thing to do..
    But the moment passed.
    He hadn't come this far to chicken out now. And not just because their need for the money was immense. No, it was because he didn't want to look weak in Liza's eyes. He knew this was kind of stupid, but he couldn't help it.
    "Do they have a dog?"
    The look she gave him curdled his insides. It was the one she gave him every time she thought he was being especially stupid or obtuse. Once again, not actually being able to see her features made no difference. He knew all her looks too well. And this one was evident in the set of her eyes alone. "I already went over this with you. They had a dog, a Corgi, but it died last year. Look, I can do this on my own. If you don't totally have your shit together, you could foul this whole thing up. Why don't you go wait in the car, be the getaway driver. I can do it on my own, no problem."
    Chip felt shamed at how tempted he was by this prospect. But he gathered his courage and shook his head. "No way. I forgot, that's all."
    Liza rolled her eyes. "What the fuck? Were you standing at the back of the line when they were handing out brains?"
    Her words stung. "I'm not stupid."
    She grunted. "I know, baby. So stop acting like it."
    Liza unlatched the gate and eased it open. Chip grimaced at the way the hinges groaned. The sound

wasn't terribly loud—it probably couldn't be heard from inside the house—but his nerves were on edge and every little thing was making him extra jumpy. Liza was right. He needed to calm down. He needed to stop thinking about everything that could go wrong and just focus on following Liza's plan to the letter. She knew what she was doing.

Liza stepped through the open gate into the dark back yard.

Chip followed her into the darkness.

3

Liza moved deftly through the shadowy maze of manicured shrubs, flower pots, and yard ornaments. Without the dim glow of the bobbing flashlight to track her, Chip would have lost her in the shadows. As it was, he nearly tripped twice as he made his way along the flagstone path en route to the patio. There were more flower pots lining the edges of the patio. Liza set the flashlight down and lifted one of the pots, patting the pebbled concrete beneath it for something. In a moment, she found what she was looking for and stood up again.

"Find the key?"

Liza held it up for him to see. The little sliver of metal glinted in the flashlight's beam. "I told you it'd be easy. That stupid bastard tells me everything. Here, take this." She passed him the flashlight and turned toward the French doors at the back of the house. "We're almost done, baby."

Chip knew she was just trying to reassure him. The truth was the hard part—the actual robbery itself—was still ahead of them. And this moment right here was the real point of no return. Once that door was open and they were inside the house, they would then be criminals in the process of committing a serious crime. There could be no undoing that.

Most of the windows at the back of the house were dark. But there was a dim light on in an upstairs room, just barely perceptible through a closed blind. Seeing it made Chip frown. According to Liza, Ken and Margaret McKenzie slept in the master bedroom, which was on the ground floor. They had two grown children who lived out-of-state and only came home for Thanksgiving and Christmas. This was the middle of June. Liza also said these people went to bed at ten like clockwork every damn night. Ten o'clock had been less than five minutes away when they'd stepped out of Liza's Pontiac Grand Prix.

Liza slid the key into the lock and paused before turning the handle.

Chip kept staring at that upstairs window.

He could feel Liza's scrutiny. "There's a light on up there."

"Don't worry about it."

"But--"

"I said, don't worry about it." She snapped her fingers, making him flinch. "Look at me."

Chip had been staring at the closed blinds for almost a full minute. During that time, he detected no hint of movement, saw no shadowy form outlined against the blind. He knew there were a million possible explanations for that damned light being on, the most likely being that someone had simply forgotten to switch it off before leaving the room.

He looked at Liza. "I'm sorry. I just--"

"Shut up."

He flinched again, this time at the harshness in her tone. "I just--"

"Shut the fuck up."

He started to say something again, but this time finally had the good sense to close his mouth. Liza fixed him with a stern glare. "Keep your mouth shut until I say otherwise. Don't look at that goddamn window again. There's nobody up there. Stay focused on me. Follow my goddamn lead. Got it?"

He nodded. "Yeah."

"Good."

She grasped the door handle again and began to turn it with exquisite, slow care, so as to create as little noise as possible. There was a tiny, almost inaudible click as the lock unlatched. After a pause, Liza began to push the door open with an equal amount of care. Chip held his breath, expecting to hear a squeaking of hinges. But that didn't happen. Unlike the gate's rusted hinges, these were apparently well-oiled.

The door was open.

Chip peered through it and got a glimpse of a kitchen shrouded in darkness. He was able to make out fuzzy outlines of things thanks only to the faint glow of a lamp spilling in from an adjacent room. He saw pots and pans hanging from an overhead rack above an island in the middle of the room. There were wrought-iron chairs along one side of the island. A table occupied a dining area nearby.

Liza glanced at Chip and put a finger to her lips. *Quiet.*

No kidding.

Chip had every intention of being the quietest motherfucker on the planet until they had this situation well and truly under control.

Liza stepped through the door into the kitchen. Once again, Chip followed her into darkness.

4

Once he was inside the kitchen, Chip eased the door most of the way shut, but did not push it all the way into the frame. This hadn't been part of Liza's instructions, but he thought it showed good initiative on his part. Leaving the door partly open would make beating a hasty retreat a smidgen easier if that proved necessary. Then again, how hasty a retreat could it be if they had to go fumbling around in the dark back there again? They would have to go around the side of the house and out through the gate again. It would take way too long. No, if they ran into trouble, they'd have to go out through the front door.

These thoughts zipped through Chip's head in a matter of seconds. His brain was in overdrive. It was yet another indicator of how on edge he was. His nerves were fried and it was filling his head with a lot of useless clutter. He closed his eyes for a moment, took a big breath, and tried to empty his mind entirely. The mental noise began to subside almost at once.

Good.

Now he could focus on the job properly.

Or so he thought until he banged his hip against a corner of the kitchen island.

"Ouch."

The word came out at normal conversational volume. Under ordinary circumstances, this would not have been a big deal. He was kind of a soft-spoken guy. He sometimes had to raise his voice and repeat himself when people failed to hear or acknowledge things he said. But now, in this setting, it sounded as if he had shouted. The pain had startled him and he hadn't been able to help it. But that made what he had done no less stupid or forgivable. Why on earth had he closed eyes in the midst of doing something so potentially dangerous? It made no sense at all.

Liza undoubtedly thought the same thing.

She turned toward him and raised a finger to her lips. The deeper shadows of the kitchen made reading her expression harder than it had been outside. He could just barely discern her eyes through the holes in the ski mask. Even so, her fury was a palpable thing. She might have slapped him or slugged him in the mouth if not for the need to stay quiet.

They stayed where they were a moment longer, waiting to determine whether anyone else had heard his unfortunate exclamation. Chip strained his ears, expecting to hear a pad of footsteps or a voice asking who was in here. A part of him half-hoped he would hear these things. They would obviously then half to abort the mission and get the hell out of this place. He needed the money in a big way. They both did. But what they were doing was wrong. Taking what didn't belong to you was wrong. Never mind the very real possibility of taking a bullet to the head from the gun of a spooked homeowner.

And according to Liza, Ken McKenzie did own several firearms, so that wasn't out of the realm of possibility. She also said he kept them locked up, but did she really know that for sure? Wasn't it possible he kept just one of them out in case of scenarios just like this one? It could be in a drawer by his nightstand, within easy reach should he need to dispatch a bumbling intruder like Chip Taylor.

Yeah.

It was *definitely* possible.

Chip's brain was in overdrive again, but now he was helpless to do anything about it. He was too rattled by his own mistake. But after many silent seconds passed, it became clear his outburst had gone unheard by the McKenzies.

He was sort of disappointed.

It was something he would never tell Liza, but he could admit the truth of it to himself. He didn't want to do this anymore. He was too scared. If it had been just him doing this, he would have turned tail and run by now. He would be in the fucking car, speeding away from here and thanking God for having come to his senses.

But that wasn't going to happen.

He did what Liza wanted. Always. Everything they ever did got done the way she wanted, and he no longer even made token attempts at going against her wishes. Many would call him pussy-whipped, but most of the time he was pretty okay with it. He loved her. Also, she fucked like a demon. The positives outweighed the negatives in their relationship most of the time. This wasn't one of those times. In retrospect, it was so fucking clear. As always, she had overwhelmed him with the sheer force of her personality. She had conveyed the basic scheme so forcefully—and so convincingly—that she'd had him believing it was a good idea. But that had been in their trailer. During the daytime. Now, here in the darkness of this stranger's house, it no longer seemed like a good idea at all.

Liza turned away from him and continued forward through the darkness toward the faint light visible through the archway at the other end of the kitchen. After a brief hesitation, Chip followed her. It wasn't like there was any other viable option left at this point.

She stopped as she reached the archway, allowing him to catch up.

He stood next to her and peered out at a short, dark hallway. A tall grandfather clock stood at the end of it. There was another archway to the right of the grandfather clock. The faint light was coming from that direction. To the left was a staircase leading to the second floor. Framed pictures lined the walls. Chip took special note of a glass curio cabinet standing against the wall to the left. It was too easy to imagine bumping into the thing and knocking it over. The sound of all that glass shattering on the hardwood floor would be like a bomb going off compared to his kitchen utterance.

Liza gave his arm a brief, almost affectionate squeeze and eased into the hallway. The short-lived physical contact did more to steady his nerves than any of her many verbal admonitions. It was a simple gesture, really, but right now, in these stressful circumstances, it was an important reminder of how much she really did care about him.

He followed her into the hallway, keeping his gun at shoulder level, but aimed at the ceiling. He didn't want to shoot his girlfriend by accident. He didn't want to shoot anyone, for that matter. If things went the way Liza insisted they would, that shouldn't be an issue.

Things usually went the way Liza said they would.

Mostly.

A slight majority of the time.

Which amounted to the same thing.

Right?

The floorboards creaked under Chip's feet as he made his way to the end of the hallway. It wasn't a loud sound, but it made him cringe each time he heard it. He told himself the creaking could pass for normal house-settling noises, but his rattled psyche didn't quite buy it. The sound came again, louder than before, and he had to fight the urge to whimper.

At long last, they reached the lit archway.

Chip stood shoulder-to-shoulder with Liza and peered into a room so tastefully appointed it looked like the kind of thing you'd see in a photo spread in *Southern Living*. The furniture was all real wood and leather. A 55" flat-screen television hung from a wall opposite a plush-looking black sofa. Ken McKenzie sat kicked back in a brown recliner next to the sofa. He gave no indication of having detected their presence. The earbuds protruding from his ears revealed the reason why. He was waving a hand in the air in a way Chip initially found inexplicable, until he realized the man must be listening to classical music. He was pretending to conduct a symphony orchestra.

Chip sighed in relief.

This was a fortunate turn of events. It meant they should have no trouble getting the drop on him. He would have no time to react or fend them off. There was no sign of Mrs. McKenzie. Even better. Dealing with them separately would be less chaotic. They could subdue the old man and then proceed to the master bedroom to bind and gag his wife, who was probably already asleep. Chip was feeling better about things by the moment. This was all going to work out fine, after all.

Liza slipped through the archway and moved into a position squarely to the rear of the recliner. Chip again followed her lead, beginning to grin as the old man again failed to take any note of them. The grin faltered when Liza slipped her gun into a pocket and removed a big hunting knife from the inside of her jacket. He hadn't even known she owned a knife like that. Its sparkling, clean blade told him it was brand new, that it had perhaps been purchased as recently as today.

Chip's breath caught in his throat.

What the fuck is she doing?

The shocking answer came just seconds later as she leaned over the top of the recliner and ripped the blade across Ken McKenzie's throat.

5

Chip wanted to scream, but a rock was lodged in his throat. Or at least that was how it felt. Blind panic and terror rendered screaming or swallowing momentarily impossible. He was unable to make sense of what he was seeing on any level.

Ken McKenzie pitched forward out of the recliner, landing on his hands and knees as blood spattered the expensive throw rug beneath him. He raised a shaky hand to his throat, perhaps thinking he might stem the lethal flow of blood, but there was no chance of that. It was coming out too fast. The hole Liza's blade had created was too big, had torn open his jugular or carotid, whatever that big one was near the front of the throat.

The rock in Chip's throat abruptly dissolved.

"The fuck did you do?"

Liza's attention had been riveted to Ken. When her head whipped in Chip's direction, he saw excitement flashing in her eyes. And there was something else there, too. *Anger.* At first he thought it was because he had spoken aloud again. They still had to do deal with Mrs. McKenzie. Alerting her to their presence now—after what Liza had done—could prove disastrous. But he soon understood her anger was about something else.

She had been enjoying watching McKenzie bleed out, and she was pissed at Chip for interrupting.

The last of the dying man's strength deserted him and he slumped to the floor, where he twitched a time or two before going completely still. Blood continued to pump from the severed vein in his throat a few moments longer, staining the section of throw rug around his head a deep shade of crimson.

Holy motherfucking shit.

Chip still couldn't believe it, despite the very stark evidence in front of him.

Liza just murdered somebody. What the fuck? What the fucking fuck?

At no point during their discussions of their first foray into serious crime had she mentioned anything about killing anyone. In fact, she had gone to great pains to reassure him nothing of the sort would happen. She told him they were taking the guns for intimidation purposes only. No one would get hurt, at least not seriously. At worst, they might have to smack someone upside the head to get them to cooperate, but murder had not been on the agenda. Liza had said so in the most unequivocal terms.

Chip's eyes went to the knife again.

He watched wet blood drip from its tip and plop on the floor.

The knife meant she had been lying all along. She'd told Chip only what she thought he needed to hear in order to go along with her scheme. Killing Ken McKenzie had been part of her private agenda from the beginning.

Someone shrieked. Chip's gaze snapped away from Liza's glaring face. A dowdy woman in late middle age stood framed in an archway at the far end of the living room. She had frizzy gray hair and bags under her eyes and wore a lacy nightgown that looked more suited to a woman half her age. A light was visible through the archway. Chip was sure it had come on within the last few seconds. The dead man's wife had heard the commotion and had come out to investigate, never for a moment expecting to see anything so gruesome as the sight that greeted her.

There was a sturdy wood coffee table between Liza and the old woman. She leapt over it, knocking over a wicker basket full of magazines with the heel of her boot. Mrs. McKenzie stumbled backward through the archway as Liza charged straight at her. The poor old gal never stood a chance. Her terror and inability to fully believe what she was seeing incapacitated her. Liza seized a handful of frizzy hair and dragged her back into the living room, where she forced the bawling, blubbering woman to her knees. She then planted a knee in her back and pushed her to the floor, forcing her to lie flat on her stomach.

Mrs. McKenzie was face-to-face with her dead husband. She reached out to him with a trembling hand. Liza pressed the sharp edge of the blade against her flabby throat. Chip just stood there, feeling paralyzed and unable to do anything but watch.

Liza cut her second throat of the night.

Chip felt sick.

Liza wasn't a perfect person. He had never believed otherwise. She had her flaws, plenty of them, but so did everyone else. She was mean to people sometimes. She could be cruel and emotionally manipulative. She would laugh at the misfortunes of others and cut down her friends behind their backs. On more than one occasion she had been physically abusive with him, hitting him when she was especially infuriated by something he'd said or done. He knew he could overpower her if she ever pushed it too far, but she never quite did. Besides, he'd never gotten physically violent with a woman and didn't think he was capable of it. Maybe if his life depended on it, but only then. Anyway, despite all he knew about her darker side, never in a million years would he have guessed she could kill anyone.

Especially not like this, with such unrestrained, almost gleeful savagery.

Liza stood up and peeled the ski mask off her face. Her long blonde hair was tied back in a ponytail, but several sweat-drenched strands had come loose and were now dangling across the top half of her pretty face. She stuffed the mask inside her jacket and zipped it up again.

She looked at Chip. "Take your mask off."

Chip blinked a few times before finally finding his voice, which emerged sounding softer and weaker than ever. "What?"

"Are you deaf? Take off your goddamn mask."

Chip hesitated. "We should leave them on until we're out of here. To be safe."

Liza laughed. "They're dead, Chip. You can relax. There's no one left to give the cops a description. Take your mask off before I come over there and tear it off your head."

Chip reluctantly peeled off the mask. "Why did you kill them?"

Liza shook the hair out of her face and gave him a hard look. "Figure it out, dummy. How stupid would it be to do something like this and let the only witnesses live?"

"You meant to do this all along."

"Of course."

"You lied."

Liza smirked. "Only because I knew you wouldn't have the balls to go along with it. Shit. I knew this was gonna be easy, but if I'd known *how* easy, I would've done it myself and left your useless ass at home."

His downcast expression made her smirk fade. "Aw, you're not really useless, Chip. I love you. I'm just all amped up with adrenaline. Let's go get the money. The sooner we do that, the sooner we can get home and start celebrating."

Chip tucked away the ski mask and followed Liza through the same archway through which the late Mrs. McKenzie had made her appearance only minutes earlier. Through the archway was a very short passage that branched to the left and the right. The master bedroom was to the left. Another room cloaked in darkness was to the right.

Liza entered the dark room and flipped on a light switch.

Chip entered the room and took a look around at a cramped office. Despite its size, the office was nice. Tall cherrywood bookcases lined the walls, surrounding the big oak desk that filled the bulk of the space. Behind the desk was a cherrywood cabinet, atop which sat the components of an expensive stereo system. Above that was a pastoral painting in an ornate frame.

Liza tugged at a side of the frame. It swiveled outward on hinges like a door. Chip shook his head at the sight of a steel safe embedded in the wall. Liza had told him about it beforehand, but seeing it was kind of surreal. Hiding a safe behind a painting was too damn hokey. It was the kind of thing rich people did in old movies. No one did it in real life. Or so he had assumed. Liza spun the safe's combination dial this way and that. In seconds she had the safe open. She reached inside it and pulled out a thick manila envelope.

The money was for a car. Ken McKenzie had withdrawn it from a money market account for the purpose of making a cash payment to an acquaintance who was selling him a used Ferrari. Only now that transaction would never be completed. Liza knew about the deal because he had bragged about it. He'd wanted her to know how important he was, how it was nothing to him to withdraw a big wad of cash and blow it on a showy car.

Liza had been McKenzie's girl on the side for the last few months. Chip hadn't much liked the arrangement. The idea of some other guy—especially some entitled old rich guy—fucking his girl made his blood boil. But the weekly money McKenzie gave her as part of the deal put food on their table and helped keep the lights on. Only problem was it hadn't been quite enough. The old man was stingy. The couple hundred a week he gave her was a tiny fraction of what he could actually afford to pay.

 It was a power trip thing. McKenzie knew Liza's financial situation, how desperate it was, and he gave her just enough to make continuing the arrangement worth her while. But not one penny more than that. He didn't want her getting spoiled or thinking she was anything better than a common whore. But McKenzie had grossly underestimated her. It was easy to understand why. Liza was poor despite her good looks, which could only mean she was not bright. One way or another, most truly good-looking girls with decent smarts were able to leverage their good looks into a better standard of living. Liza hadn't managed this trick for lots of reasons. She had made mistakes. She had a criminal record. These things made it harder to get ahead. But McKenzie hadn't known any of that. To him she was just another pretty simpleton. Just another disposable plaything he would tire of soon enough. Unfortunately for him, he had never suspected how smart—nor how cunning—she truly was.

 McKenzie's wife was gone a lot. She frequently had rich society lady business around town. So Ken would sometimes bring Liza to the house during the day. She figured he got some kind of weird thrill from the off-chance of the wife coming home early one day to catch him in the act with his nubile young mistress. Liza watched him open the safe several times after these encounters. He would pull out a stack of cash and peel off bills for her. It was another way of showing off. His arrogance and his low opinion of her blinded him to her machinations. Not once had he noticed how carefully she observed him each time he opened that safe in her presence. Memorizing the combination was easy.

His attitude pissed her off, but she played the role of the airheaded bimbo to perfection and bided her time, knowing the opportunity for a bigger payoff would present itself eventually. And so it had, in the form of the recent withdrawal.

It was the perfect chance.

That was what she'd told Chip earlier today. The safe was full of cash, which wasn't always the case. They had to strike while the iron was hot. She knew where the spare keys to the house were hidden. And she knew McKenzie never engaged the alarm system until at least 10:00 pm. She had been right about everything and it had all gone off perfectly, more or less.

Except that she had lied to him.

Except that she was a remorseless, cold-blooded murderer. She wasn't the person he'd believed she was and he didn't know what to do with that terrifying information. At least not yet, here in this house that didn't belong to them, with an envelope of ill-gotten money clutched in his murdering girlfriend's gloved hand and a couple of butchered bodies in the next room.

Liza opened the envelope over the desk and shook it.

Stacks of crisp, banded bills tumbled out.

Chip's breath caught in his throat at the sight of it. It was more money than he had seen at one time in his entire life. Seeing it dumped out on the desk did something funny to him. It opened him up to an unfamiliar kind of moral relativism. He started thinking again about how much easier life could become if they got away with this. Oh, things couldn't change overnight. They would have to spend the money wisely and not make any extravagant purchases. Things like that roused suspicion. The same thing went for immediately paying off all their debt. The smart thing would be to steadily increase payments to their creditors until all accounts were settled. But for the first time in years, becoming debt-free and solvent seemed like a real possibility. And all it had cost them, when you got right down to it, was the sacrifice of an older couple who had already lived relatively long and full lives, whereas Chip and Liza were still young. So, in a way, what had happened here was only fair. It was a classic case of the old giving way to the new, a generational transition kind of thing.

It was all more rationalization and self-justifying bullshit.

Chip understood this.

But he also knew he was willing to buy into it in exchange for a better future—and if it helped make living with the knowledge of what Liza had done easier.

He lifted his gaze from the money to look at her.

She was smiling and watching him. "We did it, baby. Everything's gonna be better from now on. You'll see."

A tentative smile dimpled the edges of Chip's mouth.

And that was when they heard the scream.

6

Liza banged into the leather swivel chair behind the desk in her haste to get out of the office. She lost her footing and crashed to the floor when she attempted to kick the chair out of the way. Chip's first impulse was to go to her aid, but someone had to shut up the screamer and it had to be done soon. Liza's tumble meant the job had fallen to him.

Another scream rang out as he came charging into the living room. A young woman wearing a clingy V-neck shirt and pink cotton shorts stood on the far side of the room. She had a pretty face, manicured nails, and long brown hair tied back with a ribbon. The sight of the bodies had triggered her first ear-splitting screams, but the follow-up was caused by Chip's appearance. He couldn't blame her for it. He had a gun and was dressed all in black. It stood to reason he was responsible for the corpses. He wasn't, of course, but trying to make her understand that would be a waste of time. And anyway, all that mattered was silencing her. He didn't approve of what Liza had done, but he sure as shit didn't want to go to jail, either.

The woman stood there paralyzed by shock a moment too long. He was almost upon her by the time she shrieked and spun away from him to head for the front door. As he chased her, a detached part of him noted the pattern of little black skulls on the pink cotton shorts. She had a nice ass. He slammed into her as they reached the foyer, making her yelp in pain as they crashed to the tiled floor. Chip pinned her down and slapped a gloved hand over her mouth. She flailed beneath him for a moment, but stopped when he put the barrel of the gun against her face. He put his mouth to her ear and said, "One more sound out of you and you're dead. You understand?"

She uttered a whimpering sound of acquiescence.

"Good. I don't want to hurt you, but I will if you don't do exactly as I say. Can you do that for me?"

Another seemingly affirmative sound followed. Chip had no feel for how she would really react once he let her up. She might start screaming again or make another break for the door. If that happened, he might have no choice but to hurt her. The situation was threatening to spin out of control. It was possible neighbors who'd heard the screams had already called 911, which meant they had only minutes to deal with her and get the fuck gone from this place.

Chip removed his hand from her mouth and got to his feet. "All right, you can get up now, but do it real fucking slow, okay? I'll shoot you if you scream again or try anything stupid."

The girl did exactly as Chip commanded, moving with slow, careful deliberation as she got to her feet and turned around to face him. He couldn't get over how cute she was. How fresh-faced, despite the tears coursing down her cheeks. She couldn't have been much more than twenty-years-old.

"What's your name?"

Her bottom lip trembled. "V-V...Violet."

Chip smiled. The smile was reflex. Something made him want to reassure her, make her believe everything okay, despite the abundant gruesome evidence to the contrary. "Here's what's gonna happen. I'm gonna tie you up and put you in a closet, but that's only so you can't call the cops. We're not gonna hurt you."

"Like hell we're not."

Violet flinched at the sound of Liza's voice. Then her eyes got big when Liza came into the foyer and shoved Chip out of the way. She cringed and tried to duck her head as Liza swung the base of a heavy lamp at her. She was too slow, though, and the lamp's base cracked against the side of her head, knocking her to the floor. She didn't move or attempt to get up. At first Chip thought she was dead. She was so still, like a fallen statue. But then her mouth opened and she drew in a breath.

Not that it mattered.

He'd been naïve to think he could spare her the same fate as Mr. and Mrs. McKenzie, who were probably her parents. She had seen their faces. And Liza had already demonstrated how ruthless she could be.

"I thought you said the kids only came around for the holidays."

Liza grunted. "I don't know who this chick is, but she's not one of their kids. I've seen the pictures. Where the hell did she come from anyway?"

Chip flashed back to those moments on the patio out back, grimacing at the memory of the light visible through the second floor window. He cursed himself for not trusting his instincts on that. They should have checked out the second floor as soon as they were done dealing with Ken and Margaret.

"That light we saw. She was upstairs."

A pained look crossed Liza's face. "Whatever. We need to go."

"What about the money?"

She patted the front of her zipped-up jacket. "Got it."

Chip nodded at the girl. "I guess you're gonna kill her, huh?"

Liza stroked her chin as she thought about it a moment. "Hmm. She's cute."

Chip frowned. "What's that got to do with anything?"

"We're taking her with us."

Chip sputtered a moment before he could speak coherently. "What? Why?"

"I've got an idea."

Chip couldn't wrap his head around what she was saying. In a way, it stunned him even more than what she had done to the McKenzies. He couldn't fathom why they might want to take the girl. Though he loathed the idea, killing her now made more sense than that.

Liza saw his confusion and gave him one of her hardest looks. "This is what we're doing. Get her up and let's get moving."

"But--"

"Don't argue with me, Chip. Pissing me off is the last thing you want to do right now." She went to the front door and waited for him. "Get the bitch on her feet. Now."

Chip knew better than to press the point when she gave him a warning that emphatic. It meant her tolerance for backtalk and hesitation was at an absolute end. So he put his gun away and hauled the girl to her feet. She was in a woozy semi-conscious condition, her head wobbling as he held on to her and steered her to the door.

Liza flicked a switch by the door, extinguishing the porch light. After a last glance back at Chip and the girl, she opened the door and they hurried out of the house.

7

Violet sagged in his arms as they reached the sidewalk, her feet skidding limply across the concrete. Chip tried to rouse her, but she was out cold, so he swept her into his arms and carried her across the street to Liza's car.

Liza jogged ahead of them and opened the Pontiac's trunk. Chip immediately intuited what she wanted him to do with Violet. He wasn't happy about it—just as he wasn't happy about much of anything that had transpired—but at this point there would at least be some relief in getting the girl stashed away out of sight.

The street was still empty of traffic and there were still no pedestrians out and about. He didn't hear any sirens or see any flashing lights approaching in the distance, indicating that the girl's screams had failed to alert the neighbors. By tomorrow the murders would be big news and the people here would be shaking their heads and saying how they couldn't believe something so horrible had happened right under their noses. But for now the illusion of urban tranquility remained intact.

Luck was still on their side. For now.

Chip crammed the unconscious girl into the tight space of Liza's trunk. Moments later they were inside the car and speeding away from the scene of the crime.

Nothing was said until they were clear of the well-to-do neighborhood. Liza stopped at a red light, peeled the leather gloves off her hands, and tossed them in the back. She glanced at Chip and smiled. "Holy shit, Chip. We actually pulled it off. Can you believe it?"

Chip didn't say anything until the light cycled back to green and Liza took the car through the intersection. "What are we gonna do with that girl?"

Liza made a face. "Jesus Christ. Can't you relax for one moment and be happy? Don't worry about her. Everything's gonna be fine now. All our problems will soon be behind us."

But Chip couldn't let it go. "Don't worry about her? How can I not? We *kidnapped* somebody. There's a real, live human being in the trunk of your car. You expect me to just put that out of my mind? Fucking hell, that's impossible. Why did we even take her at all?"

Liza made a sound of exasperation. "Goddamn, you're like a dog with a bone. I've got something in mind, I already told you that."

"Yeah. You did. You just haven't told me what the fuck it is."

Liza hit her blinker and took an abrupt right turn into the nearly empty parking lot of a little strip mall where most of the shops had already closed for the night. She pulled into a shadowy slot in a corner, as far removed as she could get them from the sodium lamp posts illuminating most of the lot.

She shut the engine off and twisted in her seat to look at Chip. ""I'll tell you all about it soon, but there's something I want from you first."

Chip's face crinkled in confusion. "From me? What are you--"

He felt a spike of panic as she lunged at him. This was understandable. He had just watched her viciously murder two people, after all. That she was dangerous was indisputable. But then he felt her lips on his mouth, warm and moist, and he realized this particular act of aggression was sexual in nature. She gave his crotch a hard squeeze and pushed her tongue between his lips. Suddenly his body was responding and all his other concerns fell away, at least for the time being.

She broke off the kiss and grinned. "Backseat."

She surged out of her seat and slithered through the gap between seats into the back, where she unzipped her jacket and shrugged out of it. The envelope of money and her ski mask tumbled out, landing on the floorboard behind the driver's seat. She then kicked off her boots and began removing the rest of her clothing.

What she was doing was incredibly brazen and risky, which was right in line with the whole theme of the night, really. They could get busted here. It was late, but it wasn't *that* late. A cop might cruise by the area and take note of what was happening, maybe suspect an act of prostitution was occurring and decide to take a closer look. And if *that* happened, the odds of getting caught with the stolen loot and the kidnapped girl increased dramatically.

Chip was well aware of all this, but he didn't care. The sight of Liza's creamy, bare flesh lit a fire inside him that could only be put out one way. The moment her bra came off and he got a look at her beautiful breasts, he set his gun on the dash and climbed into the back with her, then began discarding his own clothes. She wriggled out of her panties and arranged her body in an optimal car seat entry position, with her legs spread wide and one of her feet wedged down into the floor, her head and shoulders wedged into the space where the edge of the seat met the door.

As he continued to shed his own clothes, a vivid image invaded his mind—Liza tearing open the old man's throat with that big blade. But even that wasn't enough to squash his excitement, nor was the knowledge of their captive hidden away in the trunk. The adrenaline burning through his veins was a large part of why his ardor could not be dampened. He found Liza sexy and exciting under ordinary circumstances, but the primal thrill of getting away with doing very bad things suddenly made it feel like nothing in the world was more important or necessary than fucking her right here and now.

Finally he was naked and between her legs and sliding inside her. He gasped at how wonderfully wet and warm she was, then gasped again as she clawed at him, her nails tearing into his back hard enough to draw little trickles of blood. They made a lot of noise and the car rocked and squeaked on its springs.

They didn't realize the girl in the trunk had started screaming until several moments after Chip shot his load inside Liza and collapsed atop her.

8

They scrambled to get dressed as soon as they realized how much noise Violet was making. Moments later Liza was banging on the trunk lid with a fist.

"You in there. Can you hear me?"

Hearing the voice of one of her abductors silenced the girl's screams.

Liza thumped the lid one more time, this time eliciting a frightened squeak from their captive. "I asked you a question, bitch, now answer it. Can you hear me?"

The girl whimpered. "Yes."

"Good. Now listen up. You're not gonna scream again. If you do, even one more fucking time, I will shoot you through the goddamn trunk. You got that?"

A brief hesitation, then the same meek response: "Yes."

"Tell me you won't scream again."

Another whimper. "I won't scream again, I promise. Please don't hurt me."

Liza smirked. "I promise I won't hurt you. You just remember what I said. No more caterwauling or you're dead." She glanced at Chip. "That's my quota for talking at a goddamn trunk for one day. Back in the car."

Liza didn't wait for a reply. She got back behind the wheel of the old Pontiac and slammed the door shut. Chip cast a glance up and down the street. Though there were apartment buildings nearby, this section of the city was primarily geared toward commerce. Shops, convenience stores, and fast food restaurants were everywhere you looked. Some of them were open around the clock, which meant there was always at least some traffic in the area. He saw headlights moving in both directions. Odds were strong at least one set of them belonged to a police cruiser. Now that it was over, the stupidity of what they had done basically in the open hit him hard. He recalled how vulnerable and exposed he'd felt trotting across the McKenzies' yard. Now the feeling was amplified at least a thousand-fold.

Anxious to get home—or to wherever they were taking the girl—Chip opened the passenger side door, but he didn't immediately get in the car. Something in his peripheral vision distracted him. He turned in a half-circle and peered up at the nearest lamp post. His chest tightened at the sight of a security camera mounted on a bracket.

He felt a trickle of sweat drop from his armpit.

Liza hit the horn, making him jump. "Goddammit, Chip. Are you getting in or not?"

"Yeah. Sorry."

He had no idea whether the camera actually worked. Some places put up non-functional cameras in hopes their mere presence would deter questionable activity. But those places were mostly in seedier areas where they couldn't afford expensive monitoring equipment. He doubted that would be an issue here and he wondered whether some bored security guard was sitting in a room somewhere nearby keeping an eye on the camera feeds from this parking lot. Probably not, but he couldn't discount the possibility. And if someone was watching, Chip had to wonder what that unseen observer might have made of Liza banging on the trunk and talking to it.

"The fuck are you gawking at out there?"

Chip got in the car and shut the door. "I have deep misgivings about our modern surveillance society. Big brother is always watching."

"What are you babbling about?"

Chip shrugged. "Nothing. I'm just a little rattled by everything that's happened. It's all kind of catching up to me."

Liza patted his knee. "Poor thing. I know you've had a rough night. Saw some shit you weren't expecting to see. But in a little while you'll get to unwind and have a few drinks, then everything will start to look brighter. You'll see."

Chip nodded.

If you say so.

Liza started the car and backed out of the corner parking space. After she changed gears and got the Pontiac pointed toward the parking lot's entrance, she hit the gas and patched out with a squeal of rubber. Chip pressed himself into his seat, holding onto the door's handle for dear life as Liza wheeled out of the lot and slid the car into traffic at something already approaching the posted speed limit.

Liza laughed and slugged him in the shoulder. "You should see yourself. You look scared shitless."

"Could you slow down a little? Please?"

Liza stepped on the gas pedal, making the Pontiac's engine roar as she swerved into the passing lane and zipped past all the cars on the right-hand side of the road. Chip grimaced, expecting to see flashing cop lights appear at any second.

"Okay, now you're just being a bitch. Slow down."

In response, Liza went even faster, flexing her fingers around the wheel and grinning like a maniac the whole time.

Chip's heart was pounding. If she didn't knock this lunacy off soon, he'd start hyperventilating. "Liza. Please. I'm begging you."

Liza at last eased off the gas and allowed the Pontiac to drop back to a saner speed. She glanced at Chip and laughed. "I do like it when you beg, baby. Gets me hot."

Chip listened to his still-pounding heart a moment before replying. "I'll beg all you want if that's what it takes to make you stop acting so goddamn crazy."

The look of bright-eyed, playful excitement departed Liza's features so swiftly it was shocking. It was as if someone had switched the channel from the Cartoon Network to some dour soap opera. Her expression was sullen, her eyes hard and devoid of pity. She silently held Chip's gaze long enough to make him uncomfortable. Then she grunted and shifted her attention back to the road. "You should watch the tone you take with me, Chip."

A silent moment elapsed.

Then: "I'm waiting."

Chip frowned. "For what?"

"For your goddamn apology."

As always, he knew there was no point arguing with her. She did not lose arguments, no matter what, ever. Things would only get worse if he didn't give her what she wanted. "I'm sorry for snapping at you. It was wrong."

"You were being a goddamn baby." Liza held up a hand, turning her palm toward him before he could reply. "Whatever. No more talking about it."

That was fine with Chip. He had no wish to waste any more breath on something she was incapable of being reasonable about anyway. They rode on in total silence for several more minutes while Liza took them out of the prosperous heart of the city and into the grimmer, more rundown south side, where many of the buildings were crumbling and tagged with gang graffiti. She was going farther away from home rather than closer to it. The trailer park where they lived was on the north side, itself not at all upscale. Still, the north side was a gleaming paradise compared to this area. He wanted to quiz Liza about it, but her lingering sullenness stilled his tongue a while longer.

At one point they stopped at a traffic light at a spot where some obviously illicit activity was occurring. Several African-American youths loitered at a corner. One of them was conversing with the driver of a car idling at the curb. He passed the driver something and the car sped away. On the opposite side of the street stood a rail-thin young woman in a tiny vinyl skirt and a neon-pink tube top. She tottered on ridiculously high heels as she paced up and down the same small patch of sidewalk and tried to make eye contact with passing motorists.

Liza chuckled. "You want that tranny whore?"

"No." Chip frowned. "And what makes you think she's a dude?"

"No hips at all." She laughed again. "And look at that Adam's apple. But, hey, it's cool, baby. I'm fine with you exploring your sexuality, if that's what you want."

Chip shook his head. "No, thank you."

The light turned green. Liza kept her foot on the brake pedal. "Are you sure? Look, she's staring right at us. Come on, I know you want her. Him. It."

"Will you please stop fucking with me?"

Liza giggled as she took the car through the intersection. "You're a big ball of no fun at all. What the fuck is your problem?"

"I'm tired."

She snorted. "Right. Sure. That's just the pussy excuse you use whenever you don't want to discuss the real issue."

She was right, but Chip chose not to address it. In this case, it amounted to the same thing as agreeing with her and they both knew it.

Liza took a right turn and drove past a few blocks of subsidized housing. These particular units had immaculately landscaped grounds and were painted in bright pastel colors. It was part of an effort to make the area seem less like a place where dreams go to die. Chip thought it wasn't a bad idea. These units certainly looked nicer than their trailer park, which was a pretty junky, rundown place. But the pastel apartments were noteworthy in another way, as well. They seemed familiar, as did a few other buildings zooming past on the left, including the memorably-named Crooked Johnson Auto Garage.

"Your brother lives around here, doesn't he?"

"Yep."

Chip waited a beat. "Is that where we're going?"

She shot him a strangely guarded sidelong glance.

"Yep."

"Why?"

She didn't elaborate, at least not right away. She punched in the dashboard lighter. "Give me a cigarette."

Liza's purse was on the floor by his feet. It was a big leather thing with soft straps that hung open like a tote bag. It was new. Chip was pretty sure the late Ken McKenzie had bought it for her. He opened it and rooted around inside for a few moments before locating a nearly empty pack of Dorals. He tapped one out and rolled it into a corner of her open mouth. The lighter popped out, signaling it was sufficiently heated. Chip applied the glowing red coil to the cigarette and she puffed on it, bringing it to life. She nodded and he returned the lighter to its dashboard slot.

She blew smoke at him, smiling at the way he waved a hand at it. "Dwayne can help us with the girl."

Chip coughed and waved away more smoke. "Huh? How's that?"

She inhaled deeply again, but this time she blew the smoke out the open window on her side, apparently feeling she had taunted him enough with the first direct gust. "I think I can sell her to him."

9

Some time passed. Soon they were pulling into the almost empty parking lot of the building where Liza's weird brother lived.

He came out of his stunned silence when she parked the car and cut off the engine. "Hold on. Just hold the fuck on a minute."

Liza already had a hand on the door handle. She gave Chip a look of profound impatience. "What is it?"

"You think you can sell the girl to Dwayne?"

Liza rolled her eyes. "That's only exactly what I just fucking said." She pushed the door open and put a foot out on the asphalt. "Is that all?"

Chip put a hand on her arm, restraining her. "Hold on. Please."

Liza glanced at the hand holding her arm before leveling a withering gaze at Chip. "Let go of me."

Chip released her arm. "Sorry. I just…" He shook his head in frustration. "Please just take a minute to explain this to me. What makes you think your brother would buy a girl from you?"

A corner of Liza's mouth curled in a disdainful way, as if she couldn't believe he was being so dense. "Because I've sold him girls before. Why else?"

On top of everything else that had happened, this disconcerting new bit of information was almost more than he could handle. He had never suspected Liza had anything like this level of darkness in her, not even after the murders. "So your brother is a human trafficker or white slaver or some shit like that?"

Liza giggled. "Oh, Chip."

He frowned. "What's so funny?"

"You're so naïve it's cute, that's all." She slid back behind the wheel and leaned close to him, lightly patted his knee. "Does Dwayne really strike you as the kind of guy who could run a human trafficking operation?"

Chip didn't need to think it over very long. Dwayne was too odd a person to do anything of the sort. In general he didn't interact with other people at all. He had the social skills of a rabid weasel. He was furtive and skittish, was mistrustful of almost anyone who wasn't his sister, and generally spent all his time locked away in his cluttered basement apartment. Thanks to a monthly disability payment he got from the government, he didn't have to work. The man was the ultimate creepy loner, the kind of guy who sometimes turned up on the news after police raided his place and found a bunch of bodies stuffed in a crawlspace.

Chip tried to keep his voice steady when he asked Liza the next obvious question. It wasn't easy. "So what does he do with the girls you bring him?"

"He experiments on them. Like scientific research kind of stuff."

Chip gaped at her. "Scientific…research."

Holy shit.
"That's right."
"And you're okay with that?"
"Dwayne's hobbies are his own business. I don't have an opinion one way or another. Look, don't you worry your pretty little head about it. The girl's dead anyway, you know that. This way we get to make a little extra money."
"How much?"
"He gave me three grand for the last one, but that was a nasty old crack whore. This chick's way cuter. I think I can get five grand for her. Combined with our take from the McKenzies, that'd make this a pretty profitable night, wouldn't you agree?"
Chip didn't say anything.
Couldn't say anything.
Liza got out of the car and slammed the door shut. She then leaned down to peer at Chip through the open window. "Sit tight here. It's best if I deal with him alone."
Chip gave her a terse nod in reply.
She started toward the building. Beyond the sidewalk was a concrete stairwell descending to Dwayne's apartment. Liza disappeared from view shortly after starting down the steps. With her out of sight, something inside Chip perceptibly relaxed. He felt as if a hand had been squeezed tight around his heart and now, at long last, he could finally breathe freely again. He stared at the old building and wondered how long she might be in there, how long this lighter feeling might last. But that question had an easy answer—only as long

as it took her to conduct her business with her brother and return to retrieve the girl.

Now that she was no longer right next to him, his thoughts returned to what she had done to the McKenzies, this time with a more normal level of repulsion. The vicious—and yet very calm—way she'd used that big knife on them was beyond disturbing. Chip couldn't reconcile his long-held notions about the woman he loved with so sickening an act. Anyone who could do a thing like that with no discernible hesitation…well, it was hard to believe it was their first time killing someone. And that thought caused him to further consider what she had told him about supplying Dwayne with girls for his "scientific research." He couldn't help wondering how she went about procuring them. Did she only bring him ones who just kind of fell into her lap, as Violet had, or was she actively out there prowling around for victims? He didn't want to believe the answer might be the latter, but he couldn't allow himself the luxury of hiding from the truth. She was a cold-blooded, remorseless killer, so clearly she was capable of it.

He also couldn't help wondering how safe *he* was with her. His girlfriend was a sociopath. The notion called into question a lot of things, including her feelings for him. Were they real at all? Or were they manufactured emotions propping up a relationship based on nothing more than physical attraction?

Chip was less than sure about the answers to these questions.

But just thinking about them scared the shit out of him.

A significant chunk of time passed as he sat there mulling over these things. His relief at being temporarily apart from Liza meant much of that time elapsed without him giving it any thought. Once it began to register, he dug out his cell phone to look at the time. It was just after 11:00 pm. She had been down there at least a half hour.

Chip frowned and stared at the section of brick wall visible above the out-of-sight stairwell. He craned his neck around and took a longer look at his surroundings. Liza's Pontiac was one of only three vehicles in the little parking lot, one of the others being Dwayne's vintage white Camaro. The building wasn't a big one and several apartments on the upper floors were unoccupied. This wasn't surprising. Even by the usual urban squalor standards, Dwayne's south side neighborhood was a pretty desolate place. Dwayne only lived here because the rent was so very cheap, low enough that he could easily get by on just his disability payment. Which begged yet another question—how did a guy like Dwayne come up the disposable income necessary to pay Liza thousands of dollars for these girls?

Which begged still another question—what did she do with that money?

Aside from the meager weekly payments she'd pocketed from Ken McKenzie, Chip couldn't recall any recent infusion of significant extra cash. Given how dire things had been over at least the last year that was not the kind of thing he would forget.

His frown deepened.

Liza remained missing in action for several more minutes.

He began to get antsy and at last felt like he just couldn't take sitting around in the car any longer. He took one of her Dorals, lit up with the dashboard lighter, and got out of the car for some fresh air. Smoking wasn't something he did very often these days, after having shaken a pack and a half a day habit a couple years back. But he would sometimes allow himself a single cigarette from Liza's stash when his nerves were especially on edge, like now.

He paced a small patch of the parking lot in the general vicinity of the Pontiac, not wishing to wander too far away in case Liza abruptly reappeared or the girl in the trunk decided to start making noise again. As he walked and smoked, he heard traffic from a couple streets over, but the street running right by the old building remained eerily quiet and empty.

After he had smoked the cigarette down to the filter, he decided the time had come to check on Liza. Because while she was indisputably a heartless killer, she was also his girlfriend and he loved her anyway. Which was maybe stupid of him, but he couldn't help it.

He started toward the building, but stopped cold when he reached the sidewalk, where he turned around and looked at the car. He had an urge to slap a hand against his forehead. The envelope of money was still in the car, in the backseat floor, where it had fallen in their haste to get undressed. Yet another check of his surroundings failed to yield evidence of anyone else in the vicinity. Still, it wouldn't be prudent to leave so much cash out where anyone could come along and grab it, especially in a neighborhood like this one.

He stalked back over to the car, put his head through the open window, and retrieved the envelope, stuffing it inside his jacket. While he was doing this, he spied his gun on the dashboard, where he'd left it earlier. Not exactly inconspicuous. And a gun would make an even more tempting target for a thief than the envelope. Besides, having a gun on him would make him feel better about venturing down to Dwayne's lair. He was pretty sure Liza had just lost track of time. She was sometimes gone for hours when she visited her brother, but when you were dealing with a guy as apparently unhinged as her brother, you couldn't be too cautious.

That only left the girl in the trunk to worry about. Leaving her unguarded was risky. She might start screaming again, especially if she sensed she had been left completely unattended. In this neighborhood, it was possible her screaming would go unheard or be ignored. But Chip couldn't count on that. She might raise enough of a ruckus to catch the attention of someone who might in turn call the cops.

But a glance back at that empty stairwell made him sigh. Going on forty-five minutes since Liza had gone down those steps and still there was no sign of her. Leaving Violet unattended was a chance he had to take. He could only hope she remained sufficiently cowed by Liza's threat to shoot her through the trunk to keep her mouth shut.

He approached the building and stared down the stairwell.

It was dark down there.

Very, very dark.

He let out a breath and flexed his fingers around the gun's handle.

And then he started down the stairs.

10

The darkness at the bottom of the stairwell did little to calm Chip's nerves. If not for the faint light of the moon—itself obscured by cloud cover and the leaves of a tall tree nearby—he wouldn't be able to see at all. Broken glass crunched under the heels of his boots, shards from a bottle some passing bum had tossed down here. The glass made him grateful he hadn't worn sneakers. Some of those fragments felt big enough to have sliced through the soles. Hobbling around with carved up feet wouldn't have been much fun.

There was a door in front of him. The way it hung from its hinges—not quite flush to the frame—made it look like it would yield to a single kick. It was a wooden door with a glass window at the top. Chip put a hand against the glass and leaned close to peer through it, but saw only deeper darkness.

The door handle turned when he tried it. No need to kick it open. That was one thing to be grateful for, at least. The door gave a loud creak when he pushed it open. When he entered the dark hallway, he felt like a dumb kid in the kind of cheap horror movie where dumb kids go into creepy old houses for no good reason other than to get sliced to pieces by the masked serial killer lurking in the shadows. He told himself he wasn't being rational. This wasn't a movie. Michael Myers wasn't about to leap out of the shadows and plunge a butcher knife through his heart. This line or reasoning did little to ease his paranoia. Because while it made total sense under normal circumstances, it kind of fell apart in light of what he now knew about Liza's brother. That guy had it in him to be a new Ed Gein. For all Chip knew, he might one day provide inspiration for the horror movies of a future generation.

    Chip took only a few more steps before deciding he was creeped out enough without having to stumble around in the dark with a genuine madman lurking somewhere in the vicinity. He dug out his cell phone again and pushed a button to illuminate the screen. The meager light it produced wasn't much, but it was better than nothing. He briefly considering returning to the car to fetch the flashlight but decided wasting any additional time was a bad idea.

    He couldn't see it yet, but he knew from memory there was a door at the end of the hallway. The room beyond that door was his destination. There were other doors lining the sides of the hallway, but they weren't important. One led to a laundry room, while still others hid former living spaces that had been converted into storage rooms by the building's owner. They were filled with a lot of useless junk, mostly crap left behind by former tenants. Ratty furniture, old tube televisions with busted screens, non-functioning appliances, and the like.

Chip had gone rooting through some of the stuff with Liza during one of the rare times he'd accompanied her here. She had been certain they would discover some form of hidden treasure somewhere inside those rooms. When it didn't happen, she had something of a temper tantrum, throwing around a bunch of junk in a blind rage. Chip got hit in the arm with a toaster oven. It hadn't hurt much, but the incident was one of several reasons why he had never returned to this place. Dwight's craziness always seemed to heighten Liza's own mental issues.

When he reached the door at the end of the hallway, he held his breath and stood very still as he put an ear against the old wood and listened. At first he heard nothing, but after that came the very faint sound of a female in distress. Hearing it made Chip's heart race for a moment, but then he realized there was something off about it. It sounded sort of flat, like a low-fidelity recording. The sound repeated, a little louder this time, and more shrill, as if distress had given way to pain.

This was disturbing, but the next thing Chip heard was laughter. He was pretty sure it was more than one person laughing. And when he heard the sound again, he clearly recognized the less than dulcet tones Liza produced when she found something hysterically, almost unbearably funny. It had a high, shrill, braying quality to it. Sometimes when they watched very funny movies, the sound was nearly enough to induce migraine headaches. Regardless, hearing it now made him relax, almost restored that feeling of lightness he'd experienced during those first moments alone in the car. As troubled as he was by much of Liza's behavior tonight, he didn't want anything bad happening to her. If Dwayne had hurt her, he would have killed the son of a bitch.

He tested the doorknob, but found it locked. For a long moment, he stood there and considered returning to the car. He didn't have a clue what might be going on in there and had a hunch he was better off not knowing. Liza was fine. That was all that mattered. Now that he knew that, he could resume waiting without his imagination running wild.

But the more he thought about it, the more ticked off he got. It sounded like Liza and her brother were having a high old time. They were laughing their asses off while, what, watching a movie? That's what it sounded like. And all while he was sitting out there by himself with a kidnapped girl locked in the trunk of the car. It was pretty fucking thoughtless, not to mention infuriating. He also had to wonder how much longer it might go on. Liza didn't sound like she was in any hurry to leave.

Fuck this.

He put his cell phone away and rapped hard on the door. The sound of laughter trailed off and in a moment he heard footsteps approaching. Then the door came open and Liza was squinting out at him. She had taken her jacket off and had a beer in her hand. Her blonde hair was no longer in a ponytail and hung loose to her shoulders.

"Chip? The fuck are you doing down here?"

"I could ask you the same. Do you know I've been waiting up there almost a goddamn hour? How long is this gonna take?"

She glared at him. "You sound mad."

"Well, I guess I sort of am. How would you feel in my position? I don't want to wait forever."

She held up a finger, waggled it at him. "Number one, I've already told you to watch your tone with me. I won't warn you again." She held up another finger. "Number two, you shouldn't have left the car. That girl might start screaming again."

Chip shook his head.

Unbelievable.

There wasn't so much as a hint of apology in her voice, not the faintest wisp of empathy for having left him alone without explanation for so long. He knew it shouldn't surprise him. She treated him pretty poorly a lot of the time, but somehow this cavalier, unthinking dismissal of his legitimate complaint got under his skin more than usual.

She laughed. "You still look mad."

"And you think that's funny?"

She took a sip of her beer and nodded. "You know, I do. In fact, I think it's hilarious."

Chip gritted his teeth and shook his head, his anger making him temporarily incapable of a verbal response.

"Now you look like you might cry. Jesus, Chip."

Chip heaved a breath and swiped at his eyes. He was appalled to see his fingers come away with moisture on them. Seeing the wetness made him feel more pathetic than ever. Why did he let her do this to him?

"Why do you treat me like this?"

She frowned. "Like what?"

"You belittle me. You make fun of me. You tell me you love me, but you don't seem to actually care about me."

Liza's expression changed then. It didn't exactly soften, but it became perceptibly less hostile. "Oh, Jesus. Yes, I love you. You can be damn sure I wouldn't still be with someone as dirt poor as you after two fucking years if I didn't. But you're not the sharpest tool in the box, Chip. I'm short with you a lot because being with a guy like you is like having a child for a boyfriend. You need guidance. Instruction. And a firm hand. You get it now?"

Chip gaped at her.

What the fuck?

That was her explanation? *That* was supposed to make him feel better?

She stared at him a moment longer and then shook her head. "Tell you what. You can go ahead and bring the girl down her. So at least that part will be out of the way. That cool?"

Chip gave her a grudging nod. "Yeah. That's cool."

It was something, anyway.

She smiled. "Let me grab my keys. Come on in a sec."

She turned away from him and retreated into the apartment. Chip followed her into a living space so bizarre it stopped him dead in his tracks just a few feet inside the door. The place had changed dramatically since his last visit. It had been converted into a B-movie set designer's idea of how a mad scientist's laboratory would look. A lot of the furniture he remembered from before was missing, replaced by incubators, test chambers, and autoclaves. Two long tables dominated the center of the room. Arrayed on their surfaces were microscopes, test tubes, beakers, shakers, and other things he couldn't identify. A longer look dispelled the notion that these things were party store props. The equipment was all real and seemingly state-of-the-art. It was all plugged in and humming smoothly. The whole setup had probably set Dwayne back a fair penny. Chip knew for a fact Dwayne was a high school dropout with no formal science training whatsoever. He couldn't start to imagine a single legit reason why the guy would have all this stuff, nor how he might have afforded it all.

It was all very odd.

But the laboratory equipment wasn't what really bothered him. No, the thing that made him feel like he had stepped through a portal into some bizarre alternate universe was seeing what had replaced the assortment of pots and pans on the shelves in the kitchen. The apartment was all one big open space, so he had a good view of the kitchen from where he stood. Lining those shelves now were jars of pickled organs and other things floating in formaldehyde. The "other things" included a hand, a foot, some fleshy blobs that might have been breasts, and a girl's severed head. In fact, a closer look at a lower shelf revealed that there were *two* severed female heads.

The strange, incongruous smile that spread across Chip's face made him feel deranged.

Which, given the setting, was appropriate.

He wanted to scream, but all he could do was stand there and grin like the moron Liza said he was. Whatever he had imagined when she told him her brother used the girls for "scientific research"…well, this wasn't quite what he'd pictured.

He flinched when he heard footsteps approaching him and turned his head to look at Liza, who was smirking in a knowing way. He glanced at the jars of pickled organs and body parts again and shuddered. "I…I just…"

She laughed. "I know, right? It's a trip. Dwayne's really into his new hobby."

Chip laughed. The sound was jarring in the midst of all this evidence of horror and insanity. But he hadn't been able to help it. It was a nervous reaction, a neurological misfire unrelated entirely to what he was actually feeling.

Liza misinterpreted it.

She grinned and tossed him her keys, which he snagged out of the air with a reflexive flip of his hand. "Good to see you're loosening up. I was beginning to think you'd turned into a total pussy." She laughed and glanced at the jars. "This shit's all funny as hell to me, too."

Right, Chip thought. *Funny. That's the word. But funny strange, not funny haha.*

Actually, strange was far too mild a word for any of this madness.

Chip finally managed to tear his gaze away from the horrific tableau in the kitchen to search out Dwayne and the source of the sounds he'd heard while standing outside the door. There was a big television mounted on the wall at the far end of the room. Dwayne was seated on a sofa in front of it. He turned around to peer at Chip in his usual slimily observational way. His hair was a mass of unruly brown curls. He wore glasses with thick black frames that failed to obscure the dead look in his dark eyes. He was also wearing a white lab coat. Chip grinned nervously as he met the man's gaze for a moment.

Then he looked at the frozen image on the screen and felt the grin fade.

"Um..."

The girl on the screen was a skinny thing. Her ribs and jutting hipbones made her look emaciated. She had skin so pasty-white even a vampire would describe her pallor as "sickly." Her limp blonde hair looked like it hadn't been washed in weeks. Someone had shackled the nude woman to a wall in a dimly lit room. Something in Chip's peripheral vision made his head swivel slowly to the left, where he saw chains mounted on brackets that had been drilled into an exposed brick wall. Affixed to the ends of the chains were some medieval-looking shackles. Shackles that looked exactly like the ones in the...movie.

Except now Chip was thinking it was a home movie. He had no desire to see any of it, because he was pretty sure he already knew how it would end. He belatedly realized Dwayne was still staring right him. He tried not to wince when he glanced at the man. There was something lizard-like in that gaze now, calmly appraising and malevolent at the same time.

He gasped when Liza touched his arm. Her expression was a mix of amusement and something that might have been concern. "You okay? You seem nervous."

Chip stared at her silently a moment, long enough to become certain that hint of concern masked a subtle mockery. He began to understand one of the main things she felt for him was simple contempt. When she insulted his intelligence, she wasn't just being cruel. She genuinely believed he was a dim bulb. He wasn't at all, but she believed it, at least in part because of her obscenely inflated opinion of herself. As these thoughts churned through his head, this whole interaction started feeling like a watershed moment. He was maybe starting to fall out of love with her, a realization he was in no hurry to share.

Not here, not under these circumstances.

He sighed. "I'm just tired. I really want to get home."

Liza frowned. "I want to hang out here a while. Dwayne said I could watch him perform an initial exploratory surgery on the girl."

Chip's mouth dropped open.

Yet another thing to which he didn't have the first clue how to respond. Oh, he knew how he *wanted* to respond. That was another thing altogether. It was ghoulish. It was insanity. You couldn't want to watch a thing like that unless you were borderline inhuman. Chip became intently aware of a stark reality—he was currently in a room with two remorseless murderers. They were peas in a pod, the brother and sister. Outwardly they looked nothing alike—Dwayne's ugliness was a direct contrast to his sister's external beauty—but on the inside they were exactly the same.

Chip closed his mouth and cleared his throat. "I guess I'll go get the girl."

Liza narrowed her eyes as she studied his expression. "I'll go with you."

Chip forced a smile. "Nah, I can handle it myself."

Liza smiled, too. "I insist. I'd like a private moment with you, anyway."

A great effort of will was required to keep his smile in place as Chip said, "Sure, okay."

Liza shot a look in her brother's direction. "We'll be right back."

He shrugged and aimed a remote at the big television. "Whatever."

The picture on the screen unfroze and the shrill sound of a dead woman's screams resumed, although this time it wasn't muffled by the door. The screams abruptly cut off again as a portly man in a black hood clamped a hand around the woman's throat, making her eyes bug out as her gaping mouth emitted only a wet wheeze. Rather than choking her to death, her assailant relaxed his grip on her throat and slammed her against the brick wall, making her cry out and sag limply in the chains. The hooded man laughed at her misery. He was wearing a white lab coat open over jeans and a *Cannibal Holocaust* T-shirt. The front of the lab coat was smeared with what might have been either blood or food stains. That the on-screen sadist was Liza's brother was, of course, not in doubt. And based on what he knew of the guy, those stains were from food *and* blood. The guy was a pig in more ways than one.

Liza mistook Chip's fixation on the videotaped gruesomeness for actual enjoyment of what he was seeing. She squeezed his arm. "It gets way more interesting than that, believe it or not. Come on, let's go get that chick."

Chip nodded. "Okay."

He followed her out of Dwayne's horror house of an apartment, down the dark hallway, and back out to the parking lot. Liza snagged the keys from Chip and headed straight for the Pontiac's trunk, which could only be opened with a key. The latch to pop it open from inside was broken. She flipped through the keys until she found the one for the trunk and glanced at the gun in Chip's hand, which he'd almost forgotten he'd been holding the whole time. A stray, wild thought flashed through his mind—he should have shot them both down there in the apartment while he had the chance. Liza and Dwayne were bad people. Though it still pained him to think of her that way, the truth was getting rid of them both would have equated to doing the world a favor.

Liza frowned. "What are you thinking about, Chip?"

He blinked in surprise. "Nothing."

"Are you sure you're not contemplating some kind of vigilante justice?"

"Of course not."

She held his gaze a moment longer, searching his features for signs of deceit. "You know I love you, right? I mean, really. That shit you were saying earlier...you don't seriously doubt my feelings for you. Do you?"

He did his best to make his tone sound sincere. "No. Absolutely not."

She touched his cheek with the back of a hand. "You're the most important thing in this whole fucking world to me, Chip. Everything I've done tonight is only so we can have a better life together."

Chip nodded.

Right. Which is why you spent all that time drinking beers with your brother while you sick fucks watched home snuff movies.

It was the same bullshit she'd said before. And it still sounded just as fake.

"I know." He summoned another fake smile. He was getting better at them. His eyes flicked to the trunk. "Come on, let's get this over with."

She smiled again and turned away from him to bend toward the trunk.

Chip slammed the butt of his gun against the crown of her skull.

11

This was a thing done on pure impulse. He hadn't known he was going to do it until immediately after it happened. He had no plan at all, no clue what to do next, but he was aware enough to know his course was set. Now that this thing had been done, he had no choice but to follow it through to its logical conclusion—the end of his life with Liza.

He grabbed hold of her and slammed the gun down again, this second blow much harder than the first. She cried out and pitched forward onto the trunk. She slid off it and tumbled to the ground, rolling onto her back to stare up at Chip through bleary, unfocused eyes. Her features were slack, empty of any trace of her usual smirking arrogance. Chip was faced with a quandary. He could kill her and remove her as a threat or he could get the fuck out of here now before she could get her wits about her again.

He stared at her, his hand trembling around the gun handle.

Killing her would be the smart thing. That wasn't up for debate. Whatever her true feelings for him really were, they were out the window now that he had attacked her. She would be out for blood as soon as she shook off the stunning effects of the blows.

67

68 Kill

Chip aimed the gun at her face. His hand shook harder than ever as tears flooded his eyes. He jerked the gun away and slapped it against his thigh, cursing his weakness. He just couldn't do it. He couldn't hurt her. Well, okay, he *could* hurt her. He had just walloped her with his fucking gun. *Twice.* But he couldn't kill her. Despite all the terrible things he knew about her, he still harbored feelings for her that couldn't be extinguished.

Which left only flight as an option.

Chip bent over to grip Liza's wrists. His intent was to drag her out of the path of the car, grab the keys she'd dropped, and make good his getaway. But before he could do that, he heard a deep voice barking out at him from somewhere out there in the night.

"Yo, motherfucker! What you doing with that girl?"

A tall black man with an absolutely epic Afro was stalking toward him across the parking lot. The man wore a shiny dark-colored jacket and had the kind of thick moustache Chip associated with porn stars of the 1970's. If someone ever decided to remake *Shaft*, this guy deserved the starring role. He was a walking anachronism, a man out of time, but that made him no less threatening. He was a big dude.

And he was coming rapidly closer. "You best leave that girl alone, fool. You hear me?"

Chip couldn't believe it.

A good Samaritan? In *this* neighborhood?

It was absurd.

He let go of Liza's wrists and stood up to aim the gun in the man's direction. Rather than warning him off with a verbal threat—the effectiveness of which would be dubious, at best—he fired a shot over his head. The big *boom* of the gun's report evidently was enough to dissuade the man from interfering because he immediately turned tail and took off running in the opposite direction. The gunshot also caused the girl in the trunk to let out an alarmed shriek.

Chip banged on the trunk with the butt of the gun. "Shut up, goddammit! I'm trying to help you."

The girl screamed back at him. "*Bullshit!*"

And then she started crying.

Chip couldn't blame her. In her place, he'd be just as scared. But he didn't have time for this. He needed to get those keys and get gone before someone reported the gunshot. Gunfire often got ignored in places like this, but it was possible that Shaft-looking motherfucker had a cell phone on him and had already called 911, which meant the cops might be here soon. A report of a pretty white girl possibly being attacked and abducted by a man dressed in black changed the whole dynamic, even in this neighborhood.

He sensed movement behind him an instant too late. Just as he was turning around to scan the ground for the keys, a fist crashed across his jaw and sent him staggering backward. It was Liza. She was sneering at him and there was blood in her hair. Seeing the blood sent a lance of pain through his heart. He understood perfectly how dangerous she was in this moment, but the visual evidence of how badly he'd hurt her triggered guilt. She let out a screech and lunged at him, leading with her shoulder and hitting him like a linebacker making a particularly brutal open-field tackle.

Chip's legs went out from under him and he hit the ground with a painful thud. The jolt jarred the gun loose from his hand and it went skittering over the asphalt. Liza landed on top of him and did a very strange thing—she kissed him on the mouth, pushing her tongue between his lips for one brief, delirious, head-spinning moment.

Then she pulled back and glared at him. "I love you. I really, really do. But now I'm gonna kill you."

She surged to her feet and lurched away from him in pursuit of the gun. He twisted his head to track her progress and saw her swaying wildly from side-to-side. Though she'd displayed incredible fortitude and determination by managing to assault him the way she had, it was clear she was still disoriented from the blows to the head. He was unsurprised when she lost her footing and took another tumble to the ground.

Chip knew he had to act almost superhumanly fast. He heard a very faint whine of sirens somewhere out there in the night. This neighborhood being what it was, it was entirely possible the sound had nothing to do with anything happening here. But it would be stupid to take any alternate possibilities for granted.

He rolled over, got to his feet, and scanned the parking lot for his gun. After a few moments of frantic searching, he spied it not six feet from where Liza lay moaning on the ground. He snatched it up and ignored the slurred curses she directed his way.

The sirens were getting louder.

Still far away, but closer.

Ever closer.

The keys took a few moments longer to locate. They'd landed precariously close to a storm drain. Chip's heart skipped a few beats at he realized how close he'd come to losing them for good. Having to flee on foot would have been a real fucking drag. Before he could grab them, he heard heavy footsteps come pounding up the stairwell. Accompanying the footsteps were several loud, puffing exhalations of labored breath.

That had to be Dwayne.

The big psycho appeared on the sidewalk a few seconds later. He had a shotgun in his meaty hands and was bringing it to bear on Chip. Chip's instincts took over again. He snapped his gun hand toward Dwayne and fired a shot without taking time to aim properly. The bullet found its target anyway. A dark bloom of blood further sullied Dwayne's lab coat as the slug took him in the shoulder and sent him careening backward. Reflex caused him to jerk the shotgun's trigger and Chip cringed as it discharged. Luckily for him, the weapon was pointed upward at the time and fired harmlessly into the sky. The big man staggered to his right, wobbling as he tried to correct his aim for another shot at Chip. Chip saw what was about to happen and couldn't believe his luck even as he winced in instinctive sympathy. The big man's wobbling path took him right to the edge of the stairwell.

Chip held his breath.

His finger tensed against the 9mm's trigger, but he waited another beat.

Dwayne shuffled another inch to his right as he at last brought the shotgun to bear on Chip—and then he went crashing down the stairwell, thumping head-over-heel down the concrete steps in a series of teeth-jarring thuds. It sounded sort of like someone had tossed a bag of bowling balls down the stairs.

The sirens sounded like they were just a few streets away now.

Chip grabbed the keys and got in the car. He dropped the gun on the shotgun seat and fumbled with the keys until he found the right one. He jabbed it at the ignition slot and missed three times before he finally managed to make it slide home. After starting the car, he shifted gears, backed up, and executed a quick three-point turn.

He saw Liza crawling across the asphalt toward the sidewalk, either because she was worried about her brother or to seek the safety of his apartment. Chip hesitated a final time, wondering whether he ought to run her over. She was perfectly lined up in his sights, so to speak, and he wouldn't get a better chance.

His teeth ground together as he struggled with it.

His fingers gripped the steering wheel tight.

At last, he hit the gas and the car shot forward…but at the last possible instant, he jerked the wheel hard to the right and went around her, tears stinging his eyes and his heart thumping a million miles an hour in his chest as he sped out of the parking lot and away from Liza, away from his former life, and toward…

He gnawed his bottom lip as the Pontiac roared through the nightscape.

Toward…
Toward…
He thumped a fist against the steering wheel and laughed in a way that sounded almost like a sob. He had no idea where he was going or what he might do once he got there, including what to do about the girl still locked in the trunk of the car.

He had rescued her.

Sort of.

Maybe.

But what did he do with her now?

12

After giving some fleeting thought to returning home to retrieve a few of his things, Chip dismissed the idea as foolish bordering on suicidal. Liza and Dwayne were probably out of commission for a while, but he couldn't count on that and, anyway, underestimating Liza would not be a smart idea. She might yet manage to shake off the effects of the blows she had taken and come after him in Dwayne's car. If she *did* give chase, their trailer was one of the most obvious places to look for him.

And the one thing he knew absolutely for certain was she *would* come looking for him. The only question was whether that would happen tonight or tomorrow. He also knew she would not rest until she had turned over every rock in town searching for him, which meant he could rule out seeking shelter with anyone he knew locally. He didn't have many living relatives and only a handful of close friends, but Liza knew all of them and where they lived.

He slammed on the Pontiac's brakes as he noticed an oncoming red light a little too late, causing the tires to squeal loudly as the nose of the car slid into the empty intersection. The abrupt stop caused him to learn forward with his head bent toward the steering wheel, his heart going so fast it felt like it might leap out of his chest.

Jesus.

Chip sat back, glanced at the rearview mirror, and sighed in relief when he saw the street empty behind him. If there had been any cops in the area, he might have been pulled over under suspicion of DUI, never mind that he had never felt more sober in his entire life. The lack of flashing cruiser lights made him realize he had already come a significant distance from Dwayne's place. He couldn't even hear the sirens anymore.

After shifting gears and allowing the Pontiac to drift backward a few feet, he took a moment to check out his surroundings. He saw a McDonald's with a 24-hour drive-through to his right on the other side of the intersection. To his immediate right was a Kwik-Stop convenience store. There were a couple cars in the lot and he saw some people moving around inside the brightly lit store. On the opposite side of the street was an all-night diner, the kind of place where you could stop after last call and get a big plate of eggs and bacon to soak up some of the alcohol in your system. Unsurprisingly, a tavern was right next to the diner. This wasn't the well-to-do part of town by any means, but it was a somewhat more prosperous area than Dwayne's neighborhood.

Chip heaved another breath, his heart beginning to slow down.

The light turned green.

But he kept his foot on the brake a moment longer, because he suddenly realized he didn't quite know where he was, thus making where to go next kind of a mystery. Another glance at the rearview mirror showed a single set of headlights approaching from behind. They were coming up pretty fast. Though he couldn't yet discern the shape of the oncoming vehicle, in Chip's imagination the car was Dwayne's 1988 Camaro and Liza was hunched over the steering wheel, a look of grim determination in her eyes. It probably wasn't her—he still couldn't quite fathom her being capable of pursuit just yet—but the thought spurred him into belated action anyway.

He cranked the Pontiac's wheel hard to the right and stomped on the gas pedal. The car shot through the intersection with another squeal of rubber and then down a street darker than the one he'd just left behind. It was a residential area with fewer streetlights. There were cars parked at the curb on both sides of the road and for a moment the voice of paranoia got the better of him, telling him he'd come full circle back to the neighborhood formerly inhabited by the now-deceased McKenzies. But this alarming notion died a thankfully quick death once he saw that the houses here were solidly middle-class and less grand-looking than the houses in that neighborhood. And there were very few luxury vehicles lining the curbs here. This made him very happy. In that one very black, bleak moment, he had believed fate had purposely steered him back to the scene of the crime to answer for his sins, never mind that Liza was the one who'd done all the killing tonight.

Well...so far as he knew, anyway.

He had, at the very least, wounded Liza's brother. And there was a possibility the man had broken his neck during that tumble down the dark stairwell. So maybe he was a killer, too. But that was a thing he could worry about later—if there was a later.

Some intuition made him look at the rearview mirror again. *Headlights*. And they were coming on fast, just like before. He heard the roar of a powerful engine as the mystery car's driver gave it the gas. It sounded like a V-8, the kind of engine housed beneath the hood of Dwayne's 1988 Camaro.

Goddammit.

Chip wasn't a big believer in coincidence, especially in high-stress situations. Though it defied the odds of probability in a big way, he was now certain that was Liza back there. She was hunting him down and if he didn't take some pretty aggressive evasive maneuvers here starting *right fucking now*, she would catch up to him within seconds.

And when she did, she would kill him.

Just as she'd promised earlier. And Liza was a girl who kept her word with things like that. She did not issue empty threats. Ever.

Chip stomped on the Pontiac's gas pedal and it leapt forward, tires squealing on pavement. An intersection was coming up just a block ahead, but Chip kept the gas pedal down, knowing there was no way he could stop. His instincts told him not to look at the rearview mirror yet, to just focus on driving as fast as he could, but he couldn't help it and the lights back there looked

bigger and brighter than before. The pursuing car passed beneath a streetlamp and for a flashing millisecond Chip glimpsed its color.
White.
Just like Dwayne's Camaro. The shape of the car had been similar, too, though the glimpse had been too short-lived for certainty. But absolute, verifiable certainty no longer mattered. His gut told him what the logical side of his brain still couldn't quite accept. The creature behind the wheel of that car would bear an uncanny resemblance to Liza, but as far as Chip was concerned, that was the Grim Reaper was on his heels.

The Pontiac blew through the intersection and Chip pushed the gas pedal closer to the floorboard, causing the speedometer needle to soar past seventy MPH, a ridiculously reckless speed on a narrow residential road. If anyone came along in the opposite direction—or happened to pass through one of these intersections at the wrong moment—disaster was guaranteed. There would be a rending, consciousness-obliterating crash of metal, followed by blood, screams, and the stench of spilt gasoline and motor oil.

And death.

Certain death.

Chip didn't want to die. Not tonight. Not for a long time, even if he maybe deserved it for his part in the terrible things that had happened. He wanted to live and enjoy simple things again. He was a modest, unassuming guy most of the time, and he wanted more than anything to get back to his previously unremarkable existence. But right now that seemed like a bigger fantasy than winning the lottery and moving to a shining mansion on a hill.

    The pursuing car kept pace with him despite the hair-raising speeds. Chip knew he couldn't keep going in a straight line forever. At some point he would come to a dead end and that would be very bad news, because then he would be trapped. The only available course of action was obvious. He would have to turn at the next side road and hope for the best. Of course, that maneuver would come with its own hazards. He would have to slow down, which would allow the pursuing car to close what little remained of the gap between them. But that was inevitable anyway, assuming that really was Dwayne's Camaro back there. The Pontiac was a barely reliable beater. Though it was old too, the restored Camaro outclassed it in every way, most importantly in terms of horsepower.

    Chip took the Pontiac around a slight bend in the road and gasped when he glimpsed the next intersection coming up less than a block away. As he neared it, his head snapped to the left and an idea came to him that was so compelling he couldn't help but act on it. It was a tremendously daring desperation move, one fraught with danger and potentially deadly consequences, but he saw right away it was the only thing that might save him.

    With the oncoming intersection less than half a block away, he spun the wheel hard to the left and the Pontiac shot through a gap between cars parked at the curb, bounced over the curb, and went rocketing across a neatly manicured yard. The Pontiac's tires tore ruts through the perfect lawn and knocked over a For Sale sign en route to the neighboring yard. Chip twisted his head around and watched the Camaro blast through the intersection without turning. A wild burst of exhilaration made him grin like an idiot. His maneuver had been executed too quickly for the driver of the pursuing car—the identity of whom no part of him still doubted—to react. But the advantage he'd gained wouldn't last long. Staying aggressive until he'd shaken the pursuit for good was imperative.

By the time he got his head turned back around, it was almost too late to avoid a head-on collision with a big tree planted in the middle of the yard neighboring the first one the Pontiac had torn through. He jerked the wheel to the right at the last possible second, but not in time to keep the car from scraping along the side of the tree. The side mirror snapped off and fell to the ground, but Chip had—at least for the moment—avoided total disaster.

He kept spinning the wheel as he reached a short driveway. The Pontiac skidded into it, clipping the rear bumper of a black Chevy Malibu as he got the car pointed toward the road. Porch lights were coming on all around him. Soon people would be stepping outside to check out the source of the commotion. Chip had no intention of sticking around for that. He planned to be long gone before anyone could get a good look at either the tan-colored Pontiac or its license tag.

Once he reached the road, he turned the wheel hard to the left and put the gas pedal down all the way again. A glance at the rearview mirror showed the Camaro zooming backward and screeching to a halt in the intersection he'd just circumvented. In just seconds, Liza would be right on his ass again if he didn't press his momentary advantage. The next intersection was coming up fast. He tapped the brake pedal as he neared it and cranked the steering wheel hard to the left yet again, risking another glance at the rearview mirror as the Pontiac went into a fishtailing turn.

    The Camaro had just begun to turn into the street behind him. Liza had not yet had a chance to really give it the gas. He was sure she'd seen him take the left-hand turn, though, which meant he was far from being out of the woods. As he course-corrected, the Pontiac scraped the side of a Ford Tempo parked at the curb to the right. The two vehicles briefly snagged on each other. Then there was a loud metallic *BANG!* The Tempo's fender got torn apart, but Chip never slowed down, because slowing down still meant certain doom.

    He ignored the sounds of vehicular distress and kept his focus on the road in front of him. This was a side street rather than one of the neighborhood's main thoroughfares. His luck was in, because this meant the next intersection was only a block away. He reached it in just seconds and executed another hair-raising turn, this time to the right. Before he completed the turn, he got a split-second look at the rearview mirror and was relieved to see no headlights behind him.

    "Fuck."

    He let out a breath and barked nervous laughter. Despite the exhilaration of the moment, he understood how close to death he'd just come. He also knew he was by no means safe yet. Staying diligent was important. So was the necessity of continuing to take evasive action. To that end, he kept the Pontiac moving along at a good clip. He also turned every time he hit another intersection, intuitively understanding straight lines were not his friend. Straight lines meant a greater risk of either running into Liza again or apprehension by the police. At this point, he wasn't at all certain which scenario would be more terrifying, though he figured he'd probably give a slight edge to Liza. He took his turns at random rather than consciously strategizing. Going left here, right there, then right again, and so forth. He didn't know the neighborhood and still wasn't even certain what part of town this was. The slightly slower pace allowed him to glimpse street names as he navigated the neighborhood. None were familiar.

After a few more minutes of aimless driving, his paranoia began to act up again. He felt like he was trapped in a maze with no exit. Every turn he took just led him past more modest middle-class houses and down more narrow streets with parked cars lining the curbs. A disturbing notion took root in his head and stubbornly refused to let go, despite its obvious absurdity. This notion told him he was a dead man driving. That death-defying stunt he'd pulled somewhere back there in the night? Well, funny thing, it turned out the "death" part of the equation had squashed the "defying" part like a fucking pancake. The Pontiac had been demolished and his body was now just a big grease spot in the middle of the road. This thing happening now, with him seeming to traverse an endless series of identical, interlocking streets, well, it was just a delusion. He was a ghost driver behind the wheel of a ghost car, a Damned soul doomed to speed through these dark streets for all eternity.

He had become all but certain of his ghost status by the time he took yet another random right turn and saw bright lights appear just a couple blocks in the distance. The relief he felt then was so immense he almost started crying. He felt like a condemned man granted a last-second pardon.

Chip hit the gas again and in moments reached a well-lit stretch of city road. It was a much wider thoroughfare than the one that had let him into this neighborhood, with two lanes going in each direction. He saw gas stations and restaurants. Office buildings and bars. The name of a motel across the street caught his eye—The Bangin' Bungalow.

He laughed.

He knew exactly where he was now. With a name like that, most people assumed The Bangin' Bungalow was a no-tell motel, the kind of place where you could pay a cheap rate for a short stay, long enough to fuck a hooker and go. But The Bangin' Bungalow was actually a classier place than that, albeit one also geared toward "adult" activities. Each room was designed for fulfillment of a different sexual fantasy. There were rooms outfitted to look like dungeons and jail cells, while others featured spaceship and harem themes. Some rooms came equipped with stripper poles, others with sex swings and various kinds of bondage gear. Chip and Liza had stayed there a night for their one year anniversary.

A stripper friend of Liza's named Echo told her about the place. They had stayed in a dungeon-themed room, with Liza keeping him in restraints most of the night. In light of some things he now knew about her, that aspect of the memory killed any pangs of bittersweet regret it might have otherwise caused.

    A turn to the right would take him deeper into town. If he went that way and continued in that direction, it would be an almost straight line back to their trailer park on the north side.

    Chip waited for a break in the light traffic.

    He glanced one more time at the Pontiac's rearview mirror.

    No headlights behind him.

    Chip hit the gas.

    And turned left.

13

    A half mile farther down was an interstate junction. As he neared it, Chip eased the Pontiac into the center lane and crossed the street to take the eastbound exit to I-40. Making the turn, he glanced again at the rearview mirror. He saw multiple sets of headlights moving in his direction, but the cars they belonged to were all coasting along at a sensible speed. His goal was to get out of the city and put a whole lot of miles between himself and its sparkling skyline. Thanks to Liza's decision to gas up prior to the robbery, he could go a good ways before he would even have to think about stopping somewhere.

    A flash of insight—or another twinge of paranoia; there was hardly any difference between the two tonight—made him realize it was too early to be sure he'd shaken Liza. She was still looking for him, he had no doubt, roaring around somewhere out there in the night behind the wheel of that fearsome Camaro. Liza had a quick, agile mind. Once he had lost her back there in that neighborhood, she would've rapidly weighed her quarry's limited options and come to the conclusion he would probably head out of town. And, having come to that conclusion, what would she do?

68 Kill

Chip groaned as he continued to guide the Pontiac along the curve of the exit ramp. Interstate blacktop was coming up fast, just seconds away.

Her next move at that point was obvious. She would have abandoned the fruitless pursuit of him through the neighborhood's maze-like grid of streets in favor of trying to get out ahead of him. Chip pictured her taking one of the neighborhood thoroughfares straight out to Winslow Blvd.—the street he'd just left behind—and then down to the interstate junction. From there, she would have taken either the eastbound or westbound exit to the interstate, where she would pull over to the shoulder and kill the Camaro's lights to lie in wait for him. It wasn't a perfect plan, but it would give her a fifty-fifty shot of spotting him and resuming pursuit.

Chip whimpered in frustration.

It wasn't just paranoia speaking, this idea.

It was sound battle strategy.

The only thing possibly working in his favor now was the randomness of the direction he had taken. He had no special destination in mind, other than *away*. Liza would have made her decision based on cold logic and her intimate knowledge of Chip and the way his mind worked. She would have decided which direction was most likely to take Chip somewhere he regarded as safe haven, and she would then have gone that way.

Chip frowned as he hit the blacktop, his mind working furiously to determine whether the direction he had picked was really as random as he believed. This short stretch of I-40 would lead to I-24. Some 130 miles to the east on I-24 was Chattanooga.

Where his paternal grandfather lived.

Shit.

He hadn't seen the old man in a year and a half, but Cecil was one of the very few living relations with whom he was still on friendly terms. In fact, he had spoken to him by phone just a few weeks earlier. Liza had been right next to him on the couch at the time, texting some friend and seemingly paying no attention to his conversation. But Chip didn't really believe that was true. Liza never missed a thing.

Chip goosed the Pontiac up past 75 MPH and hoped for the best. What else could he do? It was too late to take the safer westbound exit. He passed a car parked at the shoulder with its lights off a scant fifty yards down the road. He was unsurprised when its lights snapped on, even less surprised when it came speeding toward him, an automotive great white shark slicing with lethal intent through the ocean of night. Within moments, the pursuing car was just a couple lengths back. They passed beneath a sodium lamp as he looked at the rearview mirror. He couldn't make out the driver, but the car behind him was undeniably a white vintage Camaro.

He had zero chance of outrunning a car like that on the interstate. Taking the next exit and trying to lose her again was the only thing he could do. As if to taunt him, a green road sign appeared on the right—NEXT EXIT 3 MILES.

The Camaro zoomed closer and got right up on the Pontiac's rear bumper before swinging out into the passing lane. Chip put the gas pedal all the way to the

floor and the Pontiac's speedometer soared past 90 MPH. But the Camaro easily pulled even with him. He knew he should stay focused on the road. His head nonetheless swiveled to the left to stare at the Camaro. As he watched, its passenger side window rolled down and he saw Liza leering out at him, her expression a mix of incendiary rage and manic, insane happiness. There was a gloating quality to it, too, a look that said, *You never had any chance of outsmarting me.*
    She pointed a gun at him.
    Chip knew the game was up. He might as well pull over, get to his knees on the side of the road, and wait for her to put a bullet through his head, finally ending this farce. He felt an unexpected peace in that moment. The fear of death was gone, at least temporarily. Like any other primal reflex, it would return if he allowed it the chance. But Chip thought he could face it with some level of quasi-grace if he let it happen now.
    Liza's broad smile told him she knew precisely what he was thinking. She tilted her chin at him, indicating her approval. Chip took his foot off the Pontiac's gas pedal and applied it to the brake. The orange speedometer needle took a rapid nosedive back toward zero. Within moments, he had pulled over to the shoulder of the road.
    The Camaro pulled over in front him.
    Liza didn't get out immediately.
    Chip sat there and watched the other car for a few breathless moments, a shaky hand hovering over the keys in the ignition. A rudimentary plan took shape in his head. Wait for her to get out. Then stomp on the gas and

run her down. He dismissed the notion as untenable almost immediately. The gap between the cars was too small. He wouldn't be able to accelerate fast enough to run her down. And there was a strong chance she would just shoot him through the windshield before he could try it.

No, this was just that survival reflex making its expected reappearance. He breathed deeply and slowly exhaled, tried hard to recover that sense of acceptance and peace. But it proved elusive. Every passing second brought him closer to the reality of his impending violent death. Suddenly his heart was racing and it was impossible to calm down again. Some part of him had known all along it would be this way, that anything else had merely been his psyche trying to protect him from the terrible truth.

He listened to the cars whizzing past on both sides of the interstate, carrying people coming and going to who knew where. Regular people living their lives, all of them utterly oblivious to the life and death drama playing out by the side of the road. The sound of the cars urged him to action. He could shift gears and slide back out into traffic, try one more time to get away. The exit the road sign had promised could be no more than two miles distant now.

Chip stared at the back of the Camaro some more.

He heard its engine rev.

She was waiting for him to get out.

He was again forced to take her great cunning into account. Liza would not allow him to catch her off-guard again. He could get out of the car and face the

music now, as per their unspoken agreement, or he could try again to outrace her, outsmart her. The latter prospect brought soft, humorless laughter.
No chance.
  No fucking chance at all.
  He shut off the Pontiac's engine.
  Opened the door.
  And got out.

14

Chip leaned back against the hood of the Pontiac and waited for Liza. A few minutes went by and still she hadn't gotten out of her brother's car. The delay puzzled him. She had the upper hand here. She was the Big Bad Wolf and he was her defeated, cornered prey. All he could do was wait right here and hope it wouldn't hurt too much when she finally tired of toying with him and tore out his throat.

He thought of the gun he'd left on the Pontiac's passenger seat in the same moment the Camaro's driver's side door finally opened. Liza swung her legs out, setting the soles of her boots carefully on the pavement. Another beat elapsed before she began to fully emerge from the car. The slow, deliberate movements made Chip think she might still be feeling some lingering effects from the blows to the head.

He wondered if he might have time to go for the gun.

How stupid he had been. He'd had the means to defend himself close at hand, yet somehow that essential fact had escaped him during those moments of terror. If that wasn't a sign of weakness or lack of mental acuity, he didn't know what was. Maybe Liza had been right about him all along—he really wasn't the sharpest tool in the box. His whole body tensed and he tried to psyche himself up to go for the gun.

But then Liza was all the way out of the car and it was too late for that.

Too late for anything.

She laughed when she saw him, smiling in a way that was disconcertingly warm and conveyed what seemed like genuine fondness. "Hey, baby."

Chip swallowed hard. He pushed himself off the hood and stood fully erect. He had no desire to go to his demise slouching like some sullen teenage lout. "Hi."

She threw the Camaro's door shut and walked toward him with slow, halting steps, swaying a little in a way that made her look like a tipsy secretary emerging from a Chili's after happy hour. She was still smiling, though, and there was no trace of the harshness she'd displayed while hunting him down. But her gait steadied as she neared him and she surprised him by throwing her arms around him, hugging him tight and laughing again before sighing into his neck. "Oh, baby." More laughter. "Oh, baby."

She had her gun with her. He could feel its hammer scraping against the back of his neck. Though he had no clue what to make of Liza's unexpectedly friendly demeanor, the gun's presence assured him the situation remained dire.

She sniffled. "Hold me."

Her arms tightened around him. It was a command, not a request. He complied and she settled against him, nuzzling his throat some more. For a moment, he could imagine none of the night's insane events had actually occurred. He was still Liza's boyfriend, they were still in love, and everything was going to be all right.

But then she broke the embrace and moved back a step. The wattage of her smile had dimmed some, but there was still ample evidence of mirth in the way her eyes glittered and the warm curve of her mouth. "Oh, Chip." She laughed softly and shook her head. "That was the most fun I've had in ages."

Chip frowned. "Huh?"

"Seriously. I can see you think I'm fucking with you, but I'm not kidding. It reminded me of being a kid. The adrenaline of it all, like taking the wildest amusement park ride ever. You remember what that was like, right? While it's happening you're holding on for dear life and screaming your head off, but when it's over, you're laughing and you've got this fluttery, queasy feeling in your stomach that's kind of awful and kind of wonderful at the same time. You know?"

Chip started to shake his head, but stopped when he realized he *did* understand what she was saying. And from her perspective, it probably had been just like that. He, of course, had been too busy being scared shitless to see it that way. "I get what you're saying, but…" He shrugged after trailing off, glanced out at the traffic flashing by before looking her in the eye again. "It's kind of tough to feel the same way, knowing I'm about to die."

Liza glanced at her gun, a puzzled, almost fuzzy look crossing her face, as if she'd forgotten the weapon was there at all. "I'm not gonna kill you. Not yet, anyway." She reached behind her and shoved the gun into her waistband at the small of her back. It struck Chip as odd. He'd be worried about literally shooting his ass off, but Liza seemed unconcerned. He figured it was something she'd seen done in a movie. She smiled and plucked at his jacket's zipper tab. "I really wanna give you a chance to redeem yourself."

"Why would you do that?"

She sighed. "How many times do I have to tell you this? I love you."

"You said you wanted to kill me. Back at your brother's place."

She shrugged. "That was a heat of the moment kind of thing. You *had* just attacked me, after all."

Chip frowned. His instincts told him not to trust her. He'd wounded her. Betrayed her. She would want to get even. It was human nature. But she sounded sincere enough and, incredibly, there was logic in what she said. "What about your brother. He's dead, right?"

She shook her head. "He's hurt bad, but he's not dead, at least he wasn't when I left him."

"You helped him? How did you get after me so fast?"

"I didn't help him. There wasn't time. Once I got off my ass, I ran down to his place to grab his keys. Last I saw Dwayne, he was dragging himself down the hallway. You hurt him bad, no doubt, but I think he'll survive."

Chip wasn't sure how he felt about that. On the one hand, it meant he wasn't a killer, after all. It meant he wasn't part of the same club Liza and her psycho brother belonged to, and that was something, at least. But it also meant he had a dangerous new enemy, one likely not inclined to be as forgiving as his sister.

"So what now? You just forgive me? Simple as that?"

There was a wry twist to her mouth as Liza shook her head. But there was a hint of something darker in her eyes. "No, Chip, it's not as simple as that. We're not just gonna forget this happened. You don't knock the shit out of your girlfriend and walk away clean. You didn't expect that, did you?"

He didn't.

"No. Of course not."

She nodded and regarded him fiercely. "I probably won't kill you, depending on what happens in the next few minutes. I'll have to punish you some way, but we can worry about that later. Right now we've got other concerns. Still got the money?"

He patted his jacket. "Right here."

"Hand it over."

Chip didn't hesitate. There was no real choice here. It boiled down to handing over the money or run the risk of Liza reneging on her offer of mercy. He unzipped his jacket, tugged the envelope out, and passed it to her. She tucked it away in her own jacket without examining its contents. "Anything else? You said we have other concerns, plural."

"Have you forgotten your passenger already?"

Violet. The girl in the trunk.

Chip frowned. "I guess I did."

This wasn't terribly surprising. Until a few minutes ago, he'd been too preoccupied with the formidable task of trying to outrun and outguess Liza. But there hadn't been a peep out of the girl in the several minutes since he'd gotten out of the car. She had been bounced around pretty violently during the chase. It was possible she was unconscious. Or dead.

"You're always forgetting important things, you goof." Liza's smile conveyed what looked like actual affection. "Your absentmindedness is adorable. Most of the time. This bitch is a problem, though. We need to get rid of her."

"But your brother—"

"Won't be in any shape to do his research for a while, thanks to you." Her expression darkened. "Which is too bad. He was gonna give me six grand for that chick. Now we'll have to kill her and dump her somewhere. Actually, you'll be the one doing the killing this time."

Chip's heart lurched in his chest, the almost offhanded comment taking his breath away for a moment. "What?"

"You heard me. You have to earn your second chance. And the way you're gonna do that is by killing that bitch. That is one-hundred percent nonnegotiable."

Chip's heart was going too fast. He felt lightheaded, like he might faint. The prospect of handing the girl over to Dwayne to use in his perverted, sickening experiments had been bad enough, but at least in that case there would have been a level of disconnect involved. This idea of taking a hands-on role in her suffering and ultimate demise had him on the verge of vomiting.

"I can't do that. Please. It's not in me, Liza. It just isn't."

All emotion drained from Liza's face then, her features going blank. "That's too bad."

Chip's face twisted in anguish. "I'll make it up to you some other way, I swear. I just--"

"Shut up."

Chip closed his mouth.

He knew that flat, emotionless tone too well. It was the one she used every time she was done listening to anything he had to say. It meant things were about to get unpleasant and it didn't matter how unhappy he was about it.

Liza came a little closer. Close enough to kiss him, though she didn't. Chip felt her warm breath on his face. It sent a minute shiver down his back. He had always been powerfully attracted to Liza in spite of the demeaning way she often treated him. Even now, with the threat of lethal violence so close at hand, he couldn't help feeling a tingle of arousal at her proximity. Her scent was intoxicating, a blend of perfume, the raspberry-scented shampoo she used, and the simple, clean smell of her skin. The worst thing was, she knew exactly the effect she had on him and she rarely failed to exploit it to the fullest.

"You will kill her. Or I'll kill you. What's it gonna be?"

Chip wanted to reach out to her, feel the lush softness of her hair between his fingers. It was crazy.

He should be nothing but afraid of her. But the pull was strong nonetheless. A single tear tracked down his cheek. "Please don't make me do this."

She rubbed away the tear with the ball of a thumb. "Come on, baby," she said, her voice softer now. "You know you're not getting out of this. This is how you put things back the way they should be. Do it for me. Do it for *us*. Okay?"

He swallowed and nodded. "Yeah. All right. I'll do it."

He was telling the truth. He still had no desire to kill the girl, but he would do it for the simple reason that he was weak. Back at Dwayne's place, he'd managed a moment of strength. He'd stood up and done the right thing. But it'd only happened out of unthinking, primal impulse. Here was a chance to reset things. To resume the status quo. He'd never really been the hero type anyway.

Liza kissed him lightly on the mouth. She smiled. "Good. I'm glad that's settled. We can't do it here, of course. We'll take her somewhere isolated. And I know just the place. Can I trust you to follow me and not try anything stupid?"

"Stupid?"

Liza laughed. "Yeah. I mean, I know I'm a badass and all, but one live-action version of *Grand Theft Auto* is enough for one night, don't you think?"

On that count, at least, Chip couldn't agree with her more. "I'm not up for that, either. I'm outmatched anyway, unless we trade rides."

"Not happening."

"There you go, then. I'll behave and hang close until we get wherever it is we're going."

"I'm so glad we're working this out." She kissed him again and gave his hands a quick squeeze. "See you soon."

She hurried back to the Camaro, gave him a last smile and a wave as she hauled the door open and dropped in behind the wheel. Chip just stood there until the Camaro's engine started and its taillights flashed. Now that she was no longer in his face, a renewed sense of swirling unreality threatened to engulf him. Of all the possible ways he'd imagined this confrontation going down…well, this hadn't been one of them. She was letting him live. It didn't seem possible and maybe it wasn't. Maybe it was all a lie, a final, masterful use of her considerable wiles. Maybe when they reached this isolated place, wherever it was (her failure to specify hadn't escaped his notice), there'd be more than one body getting dumped.

He sighed.

Maybe he really was being played for a chump. That was absolutely possible. But she had beaten him and there was no way out of this. All he could do was go along for the ride and hope for the best.

15

Rather than looping back toward town at the next exit, Liza continued eastbound on I-40 and eventually merged with the eastbound side of I-24. Chip still had no clue where she was going, except that the "isolated" spot she sought was somewhere outside the city. This didn't surprise him. Though he was no expert on the subject, it stood to reason that if you wanted to get rid of a body, somewhere out in the sticks was the best way to go. Maybe you could get away with it in the city, too, if you were careful enough, but doing nefarious things in an urban locale greatly increased the likelihood of your actions being caught on surveillance camera—or by a snooping interloper with a smartphone.

Liza maintained a steady speed of just a few miles above the posted 70 MPH limit and kept the Camaro moving in an unwavering straight line. She was basically doing all she could to ensure she wouldn't attract the attention of any lawmen. This was perfectly sensible, but Chip couldn't help feeling a little more anxious with every mile of road that peeled away. After all, *he* was the one driving a car with a kidnapped girl stashed in its trunk. If blue cop lights popped up behind him, Liza could just keep on driving while he was forced to pull over and face the music. And she would be doing it with sixty-eight thousand dollars in her pocket, thanks to his unhesitating handover of the money when she demanded it. She would disappear to some faraway tropical locale and he'd spend the rest of his life rotting away in a jail cell.

The thought of jail made him queasy. He'd never been incarcerated, but he'd heard stories from Jimbo, his addict cousin who'd done a few years at the now-shuttered Brushy Mountain State Penitentiary. He didn't talk to Jimbo much anymore for lots of reasons, but mainly he'd grown weary of hearing so many graphic, lurid details about gang rapes and prison yard beatdowns. He suspected Jimbo had embellished some of his tales for shock effect, but there was enough reality in what he said to convince Chip going to prison was pretty much the worst fate that could befall anyone, even above death.

Chip thought of the gun in the passenger seat and glanced at it.

That's it, he thought. *If I get pulled over, I'll eat a bullet.*

He imagined putting the gun in his mouth and squeezing the trigger. He pictured the bullet blasting through his soft palate, into his brain, and out the back of his head. He further envisioned the resultant bloody mess. All the bits of bone and brain matter flying backward, maybe at sufficient velocity to spatter the rear window.

Chip grimaced, feeling even queasier now.
All right, so maybe I won't *do that.*

Something even more alarming grabbed his attention when he refocused on the road. The Camaro had slowed down and was no longer perfectly within the right-hand lane. It now straddled a yellow line. Chip's chest tightened as he watched the car weave and drift slowly back to the right. He held tight to the Pontiac's steering wheel, hardly daring to breathe and feeling helpless to do anything about the potential catastrophe unfolding right in front of him. The Camaro kept drifting to the right, back into the lane, but as it did it continued to slow and Chip was forced to keep his foot on the Pontiac's brake pedal. A glance at the speedometer showed his speed dropping close to 60 MPH. Then down to almost 55 MPH, which made him think of a stupid song he'd heard on oldies radio a few times, some clown wailing about not being able to drive at that particular speed. He gritted his teeth and pushed the maddening chorus out of his head as the speedometer dropped even lower, below 50 MPH.

The Camaro drifted back out over the yellow line, still continuing to slow.

"*Fuck*," Chip said, spitting out the curse through his still-gritted teeth.

He looked at his rearview mirror and saw headlights behind him. They weren't close, not yet, but they weren't far away either. And they could pass through a speed trap at any time. Doom could be lurking in the darkness somewhere just up ahead. He focused on the Camaro again and tried to think of what to do—and came up empty. Basically, there was nothing he could do other than hope Liza could correct whatever was going wrong.

At first there was too much blind, reeling terror gripping him to fathom any explanation for what was happening, but after a few more moments, some possibilities occurred to him. The first involved her receiving an unexpected call to her cell phone, perhaps from her brother Dwayne, who maybe wanted to know where she'd taken his car. And maybe she'd dropped the phone on the floor. He pictured her leaning over to retrieve it, her foot coming off the gas pedal and her grip on the wheel loosening as she attempted the tricky maneuver. It was a logical, even likely-sounding explanation—except for a couple of things.

It was taking too long. She should either have retrieved the phone by now or given up the feat as impossible until she could stop the car.

Also, she didn't have her phone with her. She had left her purse in the Pontiac when she'd gone down to Dwayne's apartment. Her phone was in the purse, so it was right here with Chip. The belated realization kicked his anxiety into overdrive. Because it meant the other possibility that had occurred to him had to be the right one.

She still hadn't fully shaken off the effects of the blows to the head. He recalled how she'd walked like a tipsy woman those first few steps after getting out of the Camaro before getting herself under control, but that, apparently, had only been accomplished via a massive effort of will. He had hit her really fucking hard with the gun. *Twice*. The blood in her hair was testament to that. She had probably suffered a concussion. Recovering from one could take days. The moments of lucidity she'd managed didn't change that fact. It was possible—perhaps even likely—that she was on the verge of losing consciousness altogether. And if that happened, the Camaro would crash into the guardrail to the right or go sliding off into the median.

    And what would he do then?

    Drive on by?

    Stop to help her?

    There was some pretty simple math working against the advisability of the latter possibility. The longer he was in the Pontiac, the greater his chances of being caught with the girl. He wanted that part of the equation resolved really fucking soon, one way or another. He could drive on by and trust that someone else would come to Liza's aid. Unless she wiped out and totaled the Camaro, she might be okay.

    Or, wait, maybe he was completely wrong about that. He thought about the items in her possession. The gun. The bloody knife and the envelope filled with stolen money tucked inside her jacket. Even the dimmest cop or EMT would see how these things might add up to involvement in some kind of crime—a crime in which he would almost certainly be implicated. A helpless, hollow feeling began to take root in the pit of Chip's stomach. A repeating pattern was becoming discernible. At several points along the way, he'd begun to feel like he was finally on top of things, like he had it all under control, but each time this proved illusory. The truth was he was never going to get a handle on it. It would all keep coming apart no matter how hard he tried to prevent it.

The one lesson of value he might feasibly take away from this lousy night? If at the end of all this he came out of it more or less intact and not in jail, he was never, ever committing a crime again. Of any sort. For *any* reason.

The Camaro continued to slow, dipping below 45 MPH. If the slowdown continued at this rate, Liza would soon stop in the middle of the damn interstate. On the other hand, she was no longer weaving quite so badly. Cars whooshed by to the left and no one had to swerve to get out of her way. Chip kept his gaze straight ahead and hoped no one would slow down for a closer look at what was happening. So far luck, at least in this one regard, was still with them. They hadn't encountered any police cruisers. And citizens didn't get out on the goddamn interstate to drive 45 MPH. They did it to get where they were going in a hurry. Also, by and large, people were self-centered assholes, too wrapped up in their own worlds to bother with the travails of strangers.

Chip's thoughts continued spiraling ever downward in a similarly misanthropic and cynical way for several more moments—and then the Camaro's taillights lit up as Liza stepped on the brake. She slowed way down.

And began to pull over.

Chip grinned and pumped a fist in the air. He was finally able to breathe easily again as he pulled over to the shoulder and parked behind Liza. Getting out of the Pontiac, he glanced behind him to check that there were still no police vehicles approaching. Highway traffic remained light. The cars and trucks that did whiz by were all civilian-owned. But that couldn't possibly last much longer. More simple math. Sooner or later, a cop would come by. It would happen within minutes, at the most. So he had to move fast.

He knocked on the Camaro's closed driver's side window. After a moment, it whirred down and Liza stared up at him through eyes that looked far too glassy. As he frowned and peered in at her, her head lolled to the left and stayed there.

She groaned softly. "I feel...sick."

Chip felt a pang of empathy, as well as a reflexive urge to help her. She needed medical attention. She needed a goddamn hospital. But those were things he couldn't help her with right now, not with the cargo he was carrying. He had too little time and was in too precarious a position. For that matter, so was she.

But then it occurred to him there *was* something he could do for her. She wasn't going to understand, might even protest, but he had to put that aside and work fast. He reached through the window and tugged down her jacket's zipper. She groaned again and mumbled something he didn't understand, but he ignored it. Nothing she might say mattered right now. He patted around inside her jacket and soon his hand closed around an edge of the money envelope. The thickness of the envelope meant it was wedged tightly inside the inner pocket. He had to clamp his hand around it and pull hard to get it out. Once he'd extracted it, he stuffed the envelope down inside his own jacket.

Liza mumbled something else, louder this time, almost intelligible and with a sharper edge. She reached a fluttery hand toward the tray beneath the radio. She was going for her gun. Her shaky fingers brushed its handle and slid away from it. Chip pushed her back and lunged for the gun, eliciting an even louder squeal of protest. But then she made another, more pitiful sound, a weak whimper. She was frustrated and scared. He couldn't blame her. And he didn't have the time or even the right words to explain how he was just trying to help her. Her gun went in another pocket. He plucked the keys from the Camaro's ignition and shoved them down inside a hip pocket of his jeans. She mumbled again. This time he almost understood what she was saying. She thought he was taking advantage of her weakened state, thought he was trying to strand her for his own selfish purposes, but taking the keys was for her own good. He couldn't stick around and he couldn't trust her not to drive off again and maybe crash into the side of the next overpass.

It was almost time to go.

There was just the matter of that bloody knife remaining.

Chip reached through the window and slipped his hand inside her jacket again. The jacket had two inner pockets. He ignored the one he'd extracted the envelope from, knowing there had been no room for the knife there. But the other pocket was empty, too, a revelation that made Chip grunt in frustration. He was positive he'd seen her stash the knife inside her jacket after slitting Margaret McKenzie's throat. His fingers encountered a sticky, flaking residue that could only be blood, a discovery that underscored the accuracy of his memory.

But the blade was gone.

Goddammit.

He scanned the interior of the car, hoping to see it somewhere, but the darkness made it difficult. So he reached across Liza again to thumb a button that turned on an overhead light. He hated to do it. The light was yet another indicator to anyone passing by that something was wrong. The sight of his butt sticking out the window of the Camaro was sure to raise a few red flags, as well. But it couldn't be helped. He couldn't leave her with the murder weapon. But there was no sign of it in the front of the car. He leaned a little farther in and stretched his arm toward the glovebox. As he struggled to slide his fingers under the handle, it occurred to him he could have managed a quicker and more efficient search of the Camaro by going around to the other door. He was clearly too stressed to think straight, a condition that would only get worse the longer this took.

His fingertips were finally able to grip the underside of the handle. He pulled at it and the overstuffed glovebox popped open, spilling out an assortment of old junk mail, a thick driver's manual, and numerous old registration slips.

But no knife.

"Fuck."

A check of the back seat also failed to turn it up. This could only mean it was somewhere inside the Pontiac. Or…wait. Maybe it wasn't in either car. He had a memory. When he'd gone down to Dwayne's apartment to see what was keeping her so long, she hadn't been wearing her jacket. She must have thrown it on again after dashing back down there to retrieve her brother's keys. He could imagine her having taken the blood-encrusted knife out to impress her psycho brother. It was definitely a plausible scenario. The knife could also still be squirreled away somewhere inside the Camaro. Perhaps it was under one of the seats. But he wasn't about to tear the car apart looking for it. He'd wasted enough time as it was.

He cupped Liza's chin in a palm and lifted her head. She blinked slowly and tried hard to focus on him, but she still looked like she was in a deep fog. He could only hope his words would penetrate. "Sorry, but I gotta go. I'm not ripping you off. I'm not stranding you to be mean. Okay? I'm taking some stuff only to protect you. I'll be in touch as soon as I can."

She touched his hand. Her fingers felt cold.

Chip meant to go then, but he hesitated a moment longer.

Then he dipped his head through the open window again and kissed her on the mouth. "I love you."

She mumbled something that sounded like reciprocation.

Chip gave her hand a squeeze. After a moment he let go of her and reached toward the dash one more time to turn on the Camaro's hazard lights. Then he hurried back to the Pontiac, jerked the door open, and dropped in behind the wheel. He gave the ignition key a twist and stomped on the gas pedal after a cursory glance at his mirrors. There were other cars coming up fast. He checked his rearview mirror again as soon as the Pontiac crested the speed limit.

He saw flashing police lights. A cop cruiser was parked at the side of the road somewhere behind him.

16

Chip felt bad about leaving Liza behind for perhaps as long as a full minute. With a bit of effort, he might have been able to haul her out of the Camaro and get her situated inside the Pontiac. It would have been risky, but there might have been just enough time to get it done before the arrival of that cop. There had been all sorts of good reasons for not doing that, most importantly her urgent need for medical attention. It was why he had turned on the hazard lights. Still, abandoning her by the side of the road in that condition ate at him.

The feeling subsided once he was another couple miles down the road. By then he was able to dismiss the reflexive pangs of regret as counterproductive. It was done and there was no taking it back. It was also very much for the best. He'd done the right thing. And the right thing now was to focus on what to do next.

Which was…what?

He frowned as he realized he again had no clue what his next move was. Before Liza caught up to him, he'd planned on releasing Violet. Saving her had been the whole point of his unplanned act of rebellion. But that had been before those moments of reconciliation with Liza back there on I-40. Despite his good intentions, he'd experienced some regret for the impetuous thing he'd done. Resigning himself to the necessity of Violet's death hadn't been easy, but he'd reluctantly accepted the apparent futility of any other course.

He did *not*, under any circumstances, want to go to jail. And he almost certainly *would* go to jail if he released the girl. She would have no reason not to identify him as present at the scene when the McKenzies were murdered. She might feel some initial gratitude for sparing her life, but Chip didn't doubt she would eventually tell the cops everything she knew. Once she was safely away from her abductors, there would be no downside to it. And human nature being what it was, it was also likely gratitude would turn to anger. She'd been kidnapped and threatened, basically put through hell.

Chip shifted in his seat and gripped the steering wheel tighter as his train of thought began to steer him toward a grim inevitability.

He would have to kill her.

Fuck.

He didn't know if he could do it. Nearly killing Dwayne had been an act of self-defense, a very different thing altogether from cold-blooded murder. Sure, he'd told Liza he would do it in exchange for a second chance. It would have been difficult and horrible, but it was possible he could have done it with her around. Liza was strong and confident. He would have drawn strength from her, maybe enough to overcome his misgivings. Killing the girl on his own would be the hardest thing he'd done by a long shot, maybe next to impossible.

He tried to picture himself aiming a gun at her tear-streaked face…and then pulling the trigger. The image made him grimace. But he kept thinking about it and, as the miles rolled away, his resurrected feelings of warmth for Liza gave way to a resurgence of the horror he'd felt in the aftermath of the bloodshed earlier in the evening.

A simple truth dawned on him.

She's ruined my life.

It was true. If he went through with killing Violet, he would never be the same. If he let her go, his days as a free man were numbered. No matter how things played out, drastic, irrevocable change was unavoidable, thanks to Liza. If she hadn't murdered those people, they would be looking at a much less grimmer set of consequences.

He frowned.

Unless…

A hand came away from the steering wheel to pat the front of his jacket. The wheels in his head began to turn in new directions as he felt the shape of the envelope through the leather. He had seen stealing the money as a shot at a life free of the crushing burden of overwhelming debt. Money meant freedom. It also created new opportunities when utilized properly. In this case, maybe it could buy discretion.

According to Liza, Violet wasn't related to the McKenzies. She might be wrong about that. Maybe she wasn't one of the kids, but it was possible she was some other relation. But it was also possible she was another of Ken McKenzie's girls on the side. Why the man would have one of his mistresses in the house when his wife was home, Chip did not know, but it wasn't completely out of the question. And if the girl *was* one of his mistresses, it was safe to assume her sole motivation for banging him was money. The silence of someone like that could possibly be bought for the right price.

A good chunk of the wad he was carrying might do it. Say...half of it. It would hurt to let that much money go, but the peace of mind it would buy would be more than worth it. And with $34,000 left over, he and Liza could still get out from under their debt and have a decent little chunk left over.

Chip relaxed some and drummed his thumbs on the steering wheel. He had made his decision. Now all he had to do was find some remote spot where he could open the trunk and pitch his proposal to Violet unobserved. That would require getting out of Davidson County and away from the city. He didn't know for sure where Liza had been leading him, but he knew the outlying counties reasonably well and could make an educated guess. Rutherford County was another twenty miles straight down I-24. There were some very lightly traveled—especially at this hour—rural back roads that could take him somewhere perfect for what he had in mind.

With a plan of action settled on, he shifted his focus to driving. He had a few gut-wrenching moments a few miles farther down the road when a THP cruiser appeared in the lane next to him and lingered there a moment before driving on by. Chip squinted into the darkness ahead of him and didn't let out a breath until he saw the cruiser's blinker light come on as the highway patrolman prepared to take an exit. When the cruiser left the interstate, Chip almost sobbed with relief.

His relief was almost as intense when he took the third Rutherford County exit some ten minutes later. He steered the Pontiac through the outskirts of a smallish town called Smyrna until he reached one of those dark back roads. Traveling along the road's swooping planes could be harrowing in broad daylight, but in the pitch blackness of night, it was nothing short of terrifying. There were no streetlamps to light the way and sometimes the road curved and dipped so dramatically it was like being on a roller coaster, a sensation he'd experienced far too many times already tonight. Eventually the road carried him away from Smyrna and in the direction of the slightly larger city of Murfreesboro. But instead of going all the way into Murfreesboro, he took a turn off that back road and down a narrow, unpaved access road.

At the end of the access road was a rental house owned by Echo, Liza's stripper friend. The house was currently between tenants. It was isolated and surrounded on all sides by a dense expanse of woods. Chip had a hunch Liza had been headed here to get rid of Violet. He had only been out here one other time and had not been at all certain he could find it again. Rather than racking his already tortured brain in an attempt to precisely remember the right way to go, he'd shut off his mind entirely, allowing his instincts to guide him. Yeah, it'd been a big gamble, but no more so than many others he'd taken. And the risk he'd taken seeking out the place no longer mattered, because for once his instincts had steered him right.

68 Kill

The house had a circular gravel driveway that passed in front of the porch and looped back toward the access road. Chip parked the Pontiac alongside the porch, grabbed his gun, and got out. He approached the trunk with tremendous trepidation, his mind buzzing with an array of predictable second thoughts.

The girl couldn't be trusted, regardless of how much money he offered her.

It sucked, but Liza was right—she had to die.

Chip closed his eyes and took a deep breath.

After slowing exhaling it, he banged a fist on the trunk. "Violet! Wake up!"

17

After some twenty seconds elapsed with no response, Chip banged on the trunk lid again. "Violet, it's okay. I'm not gonna hurt you."

Maybe.

Still no response.

Chip's anxiety kicked in again. The girl had been through a lot, the occasionally very bumpy ride in the Pontiac's trunk being the least of it. Liza had whacked her upside the head pretty good with the base of that lamp. Given the significant problems Liza had experienced after her own head injury, it was reasonable to assume Violet was in bad shape. She might even be dead.

Chip hammered on the trunk yet again. "*Violet!*"

Nothing.

Goddamn.

His anxiety ebbed a little when he realized there was one small upside to Violet's possible death. It meant any decision regarding what to do about her would be completely out of his hands. That wouldn't be the worst thing ever. Just as his thoughts were turning to the subject of corpse disposal, a faint sound emanated from the trunk. A moment later, it came again. This time he recognized it as very soft, almost inaudible whimpering. Relief rendered him momentarily weak in the knees and he sagged against the back of the Pontiac, bracing his fists on the trunk lid as he blinked back tears. He was so glad she was alive.

"Violet, I know you don't know me. I know you have good reason to fear me. But you have to believe I truly wish you no harm. My female friend isn't here. She can't hurt you again. I'm going to open this trunk. Please don't freak out when I do. I want to have a calm talk about how we can maybe help each other find a way out of this shit. Okay?"

A quiet few seconds passed.

Then Violet sniffled and said, "Okay."

When Chip opened the trunk, she squinted up at him and sucked in a breath at the sight of the gun clutched in his hand. She didn't look as banged up as he'd expected. Her long brown hair was in a state of disarray, the ribbon that had been holding it back having come loose at some point. She brushed it back from her face, lifted her head, and craned her neck around to check out the surroundings. Chip couldn't help the way his gaze lingered on her body's sweet curves, particularly the swell of her hips and the distracting jut of her breasts against the thin fabric of that clingy shirt. The creamy flesh of her long, bare legs made him ache in a way he knew was inappropriate. So, too, did the tight pink shorts with the pattern of black skulls. The desire was something he couldn't help. It was aroused by her beauty and the skimpiness of her attire. It was nothing but base male instinct. He knew this but felt shame nonetheless because of a very simple truth—she was a victim and he was a criminal with a gun.

It made him feel like a creep. On the plus side, if she recognized the nature of his scrutiny, she wasn't showing it. She still seemed dazed. Given what she had been through, anything else would have surprised the hell out of him. Chip decided putting the gun away was the thing to do. It would make him seem less threatening, maybe more trustworthy.

He put the gun in a jacket pocket and extended a hand to her. "Come on, let's get you out of there."

Violet stared at his hand and studied it a moment. Then she made eye contact with him. She didn't say anything, but Chip figured she was trying to get a read on him. He made his expression as open and sincere as he could and in another moment she reached for his hand. His heart beat a little faster when her soft fingers slid into his palm. Skin contact with an attractive female was always a heady sensation, but for reasons he didn't fully understand the feeling was more pronounced than usual this time. The corners of her mouth lifted a little as he began to gently guide her out of the trunk. The smile troubled him almost as much as his inappropriate arousal. It told him she might not be as oblivious to her effect on him as she'd at first seemed.

This was confirmed shortly after she was out of the trunk and had her feet firmly on the ground. She wrapped her arms around him in a tight embrace of apparent gratitude and put her mouth against his neck, allowing him to feel her lips on his flesh for a moment before saying, "Thank you."

Chip kept his arms by his sides, not trusting himself to touch her. But when she flexed her arms against him, nudging him to return the embrace, he lifted his hands and very lightly touched her back. She shifted against him, angling a soft thigh between his legs. Chip groaned and she laughed softly when she felt his hard-on.

Then one of her hands came away from his back and pushed into the pocket where he'd stashed his gun. Her fingers closed around its handle and began to pull it out. Chip realized what was happening and made a grab for her wrist as the gun's hammer snagged on the pocket's inner lining. She yelped in frustration, made a fist of her right hand, and slugged him in the jaw. The blow wasn't a crippling one, but its real purpose was to distract him and at that it worked spectacularly well. She jerked at the gun again and tore it loose before his fingers could close around her wrist.

Violet backpedaled and pointed the barrel of the gun at his face.

Chip held up his hands and backed up a step. "Whoa, hold on."

He was glad Liza couldn't see him now because she would be giving him all kinds of hell for letting his guard down. He'd done a lot of dumb things tonight, but allowing the girl to get close to him before he was sure he could trust her was near the top of the list.

Her mouth curled in a vicious sneer. "Get on your knees."

"What?"

"You heard me. On your fucking knees. *Now!*"

"Look, you need to calm down. We've got a lot to talk about."

She shook her head. "You're a goddamn murderer. We don't have shit to discuss, you fucking scumbag."

"But--"

She took a quick step toward him and smacked the butt of the gun against the bridge of his nose. He staggered backward a step and then sank to his knees. This was surrender to temporarily overwhelming pain rather than a conscious decision to obey her command. Chip didn't believe she'd quite managed to break his nose, but it hadn't been for lack of effort.

Violet put the barrel of the gun against his forehead.

He glanced up at her. "Please…"

She smiled. "I'm a happy girl. Know why?"

Chip shook his head. "No."

"Because this is the part where you die."

She squeezed the 9mm's trigger.

18

The perplexed look on Violet's face when the gun failed to fire explained why Chip's brains were still inside his skull where they belonged rather than spattered all over the ground. She knew nothing about guns, had probably never even held one until now.

Violet's look of confusion became more pronounced as she turned the gun around to stare straight down its barrel. Watching her attempt to puzzle out the problem was almost amusing, but Chip knew there was no time to waste. He had a tiny window of opportunity here. Even someone as clueless about guns as Violet would soon figure out how to work the safety, which he dimly remembered putting on during his flight from Dwayne's place.

Chip surged to his feet and lunged at her. She yelped and the gun slipped from her grasp, landing at Chip's feet on the gravel driveway. He clamped his hands around Violet's slender neck and kicked the gun away. She emitted a strangled wheeze and flailed at him, clawing at his face with her fingernails. He slapped her hands away and blocked an attempt to knee him in the nuts. He then seized her by the wrists and pushed her backward, bracing her against the Pontiac's rear bumper to hold her relatively still.

Violet spat in his face.

Chip sighed and allowed the spittle to roll slowly down his cheek. "Please try to calm down. I really don't want to hurt you."

She smiled. "Right. That explains the gun. All pacifists carry them these days. I hear it's the hip, ironic thing to do in that crowd."

Chip frowned. "Please tell me you're not always this sarcastic. I might have to put you back in the trunk."

Her smile took on a lascivious tinge. "Go ahead. I like it when big, strong men restrain me. You should pull my shorts off and bend me over this POS ride of yours, really put me in my place."

Chip grunted. "You're too much."

She laughed. "That's what they all say."

Violet wouldn't stay still. She kept squirming around in his grip and pushing herself against him. Chip figured the constant writhing was a renewed attempt to exploit her sex appeal, but he wasn't about to fall for that trick a second time. Still, her persistence presented a significant problem. He couldn't restrain her forever, regardless of his superior strength. Putting her back in the trunk was becoming a more attractive option with each passing second. Despite the big knock to the head she'd taken earlier, she wasn't displaying any of the concussion symptoms that had taken Liza out of the game. If anything, she seemed almost hyperaware, completely focused and in the moment in a way that made her even more dangerous.

She grinned in a boldly knowing way, as if she could see through his skull and read his thoughts as easily as words printed on paper. "Oh, am I too much woman for you, sweetheart? Am I too hot to handle?"

Chip frowned. "What's wrong with you?"

Violet affected a look of mock innocence, one eyebrow going up in an exaggeratedly arch way. "Why, what ever could you mean?"

Chip didn't respond. She wasn't acting at all like a woman whose life had been in danger much of the night. Interestingly, the squirming began to subside the longer he silently studied her features. After several more moments of this, his gaze flicked helplessly to her plump bottom lip for a second before he made himself resume looking into her eyes. But the slip didn't go unnoticed.

Violet bit down on the succulent-looking lip and soon ceased her struggles altogether. "I'm not afraid of you."

"Why not?"

"It's like you said, your girlfriend's not here. She's the dangerous one, not you. I don't know exactly what all's been going on since you put me in the trunk, but I've got a pretty good idea about some of it." She smiled. "You tried to rescue me. Right?"

"I guess I did. It didn't go too well, though."

Violet shrugged and took a pointed look around at the dark woods surrounding the empty house. "I don't know about that. Looks like it worked out just fine."

Chip opened his mouth to refute that, but the words didn't materialize. He meant to tell her about how Liza's concussion symptoms were the only reason she wasn't dead now. But it abruptly struck him how counterproductive that would be, given the shifting circumstances. It would be better by far to let her believe he'd never had anything but her safety in mind.

He frowned. "Okay, maybe you have a point there. But then why the aggression? Only reason *I'm* not dead now is you didn't know how to work a safety."

"Just because you rescued me doesn't mean I can trust you." Violet's expression became more somber as she abandoned the game-playing in favor of plain honesty. "You *did* murder the McKenzies, after all."

"I didn't--"

She snorted dismissively. "Oh, please. Maybe you didn't cut their throats personally, but you were there and that makes you just as responsible as that blonde bitch."

Chip grimaced. "I didn't know she would do that. If I had--"

"They'd still be dead." She sneered. Despite the hostility, Chip found the twist of her mouth staggeringly sexy. This made him feel hopelessly inept. How could he hope to effectively reason or bargain with a woman like this? "I get that she's the boss in your relationship. But you have a brain. You can think for yourself, can't you? You could have said no to the whole thing, whatever it was. But, no, you want into that house with weapons. With guns. With fucking *knives*."

It had been just one knife, and he hadn't even known Liza had it with her until she was using it to open Ken McKenzie's throat, but Chip realized this wasn't a point worth clarifying. It would make Violet's argument no less damning. Instead he said, "Who are you to the

McKenzies, anyway? Liza says you're not one of their kids."

Violet tilted her head a little. "Is that your girlfriend's name? Liza?"

"Yeah."

"Well, Liza's right. I'm not the daughter of the people you killed. I'm not related to them at all."

"So…again, who the fuck are you? What were you doing at their house?"

Violet's expression hardened. "I'm not saying another word until you let go of me."

Chip said nothing as he held onto her a moment longer. He tried to keep his face blank, but inwardly he was stinging from her words and her accusatory glare. A faint part of him wanted to argue his own complicity in the murders further, but in his heart he knew she was right. He relinquished his grip on her wrists and moved back a step.

Violet gave him an appraising look. "I guess maybe I'm being a little too hard on you." She laughed at his confused expression. "Don't get the wrong idea. I don't mean that you're blameless. It's just that now I get how easy you are to push around. You're really sort of a simple guy, aren't you? I bet without Liza you'd have a hard time getting out the door every morning with your shoes tied and your shirt on right side out. Am I right?"

"You're calling me stupid."

Violet shrugged. "You said it, not me."

The belittling of his intelligence hit a little too close to home. Liza treated him like this all the time. He put up with it because he loved her and had a history with her. She was a kinky little sadist who got off on degrading him and, truthfully, he sort of got off on it, too. It rankled a lot of the time, but the benefits—primarily in the form of explosively awesome sex—made the surrender of some of his pride worth it.

But this woman, attractive though she was, was not Liza.

"You can't talk to me like that."

"Oh, yeah?"

He nodded. "Yeah."

She tugged at his jacket's zipper tab. "Then you should do something about it. Maybe shut my stupid little mouth."

She bit her bottom lip and stared up at him with her very big eyes.

Chip swallowed hard.

It would be easy to get lost in those eyes. Far too easy. He was tired of being so effortlessly manipulated by attractive women. What she'd said earlier was right. He did have a brain of his own. It was high time he started using it again. He heaved a breath and took a few deliberate backward steps. "I'm done with the games, girl."

Violet said nothing. Instead she whistled a few bars of a haunting tune that sounded vaguely familiar.

Chip frowned. "The fuck is that?"

Violet smiled. "One of my favorite songs. 'Look At Your Game, Girl' by Charles Manson. You know it?"

Chip scanned the ground for the gun and scooped it up after he spotted it. Violet stayed where she was and whistled a few more bars of the song. Chip approached

68 Kill

her again and displayed the gun for her, turning it so she could see it from the side. "See this button here?" She lifted her chin and appeared to focus on the indicated button. Then she met his gaze and smiled.

"Okay."

"That's the safety. You couldn't kill me because it was on. But push it like this..." He held the gun a little closer so she couldn't miss what he was showing her. "Now the safety is off. Now the gun can kill."

He pointed the 9mm at her forehead.

She smiled.

Chip smiled, too. "What do you think about that, Violet?"

She whistled one more bar of the song and shrugged. Then she looked Chip in the eye and said, "I think you can either put a bullet in my head...or you can take me in that house and fuck me like you want to."

19

A search of the porch and the immediate vicinity failed to turn up a spare key. Chip checked under the doormat, under a big rock next to the porch, and along windowsills. Violet made no attempt to aid him in the search, opting instead to lean against the car and watch him with a bemused smile.
"So I'm guessing this isn't your house?"
Chip knelt in the grass beneath the window to the left of the porch and carefully patted the ground, continuing the search even after he had begun to feel like a fool. The theoretical hidden spare key probably didn't exist. Or, if it did, it wasn't hidden in any obvious place. Nor was it lurking in the tallish grass after falling from a windowsill.
He got to his feet with a grunt and looked at her. "What was your first clue?"
She rolled her eyes and ignored the question. "So why bring me here, if this isn't your place?"
Chip gave the front of the house a moment's further scrutiny before replying. There were curtains over the windows and no lights were on inside. The "For Rent" sign in the yard strongly suggested no one was currently living here. He knew Liza's stripper friend was kind of a cheapskate when it came to the upkeep of the

house, which meant there was little chance an active alarm system was in place. It was also extremely unlikely any prospective renters would show up to check the place out at this hour. A glance up the long driveway and down the narrow access road reinforced the totality of their isolation.

    He looked at Violet. "We could break in."

    She shook her head and made a clucking sound of mock disapproval, but then she began to smile. "Oh my, breaking and entering. You must really want me."

    Chip didn't know what to say to that, mostly because the answer was obvious, so he said nothing. He stared at Violet and his imagination supplied him with a singularly compelling image of her leaning naked against the Pontiac, her lean and flawless body bathed in moonlight. Her smile took on a sly quality and he again got the impression she knew his every thought, but he no longer cared about that. He couldn't figure her out at all. She wasn't scared. She laughed when she should be crying or screaming or pleading to be let go. He was no longer restraining her or threatening her in any way, but she made no move to run. Virtually every aspect of her behavior was inexplicable, but he no longer cared about any of that, either. This whole evening had been nothing but one long, mind-bending tumble down an endless rabbit hole and by this point he had become numb to the weirdness. He had no idea how he might ultimately resolve the Violet situation and he didn't know how long it'd be before he saw Liza again. He was in a situation that had spun hopelessly out of control, one that had caused him a ton of anxiety and grief, but for now all he felt was a strange calm.

He went to Violet and there was something in his expression that made her smile change subtly, reflecting lust rather than bemusement. She opened her arms and took him unhesitatingly into her embrace. She squealed when he slammed her ass against the car and began to hungrily kiss her. He was consumed with need for her in a way that shocked him, considering he'd last had sex just a couple hours earlier. There was something in the wanton way Violet looked at him that inflamed his arousal like nothing else had in some time. It reminded him of the electricity he'd felt often in the early days with Liza—and sometimes still did—but even that paled compared to what he was experiencing now.

She took the gun out of his jacket pocket and put the barrel under his chin. "Bang."

She laughed.

Chip took the 9mm from her and set it on the Pontiac's hood. He shrugged his jacket off and let it fall to the ground, scarcely thinking of the envelope full of cash wedged inside one of its inner pockets. The only thing in his world right now was this intoxicating girl. She was sex incarnate, lust personified. She stirred strange things in him, powerful feelings that were part lust and part nameless yearning. He slid his fingers inside the elastic band of her pink cotton shorts and knelt before her to slide them down her shapely legs. She wasn't wearing panties. He slid his hands up the backs of her legs and looked up at her. "You wanted me on my knees, right?"

Violet nodded. "That's right." She put a palm against the back of his head and pressed him to her sex. "Stay down there until I say you're done."

He went to work on her and before long she was moaning and squirming against the Pontiac's fender. Moans soon gave way to panting breaths and orgasmic shrieks that reverberated in the clearing surrounding the house. In a while, she gave him permission to come up for air. When he did, he gripped her by her slim waist and turned her around, bending her over the hood of the car just as she'd suggested a little while ago. She screamed and clawed at the Pontiac's hood, urging him to fuck her even harder, a command he did his best to obey. Before it was done, he did some screaming of his own. All conscious thought was wiped away in those final moments of their ferocious coupling. He exploded inside her without even thinking to pull out, an event that triggered her loudest scream of the night. Somewhere out there in the night an animal howled in response. Chip fell panting against Violet, pinning her to the Pontiac's hood.

They stayed like that for maybe three or four full minutes, both of them breathing hard and not uttering a word. Though his seed was spent, he stayed rigid inside her the whole time. Once or twice she shifted against him and whimpered a little. Finally, she let out a little sigh and gave him a nudge in the ribs with an elbow.

After climbing off her, Chip pulled his jeans up and couldn't help noting how rubbery his legs felt. He felt like he'd run a damn marathon. Sex with Liza often left him feeling similarly enervated. She was an amazing lay in every way, the best of his life…until now. The thought made him frown. He knew he should feel guiltier than he did. This was the first time in his two years with Liza that he'd ever cheated on her. He frowned harder, wondering if it meant his feelings for Liza really had irrevocably changed, after all.

Violet at last peeled herself off the car and stooped to pull up her shorts. When she turned around to face Chip, she was smiling in that lascivious, half-smirking way he was beginning to suspect was her default expression when dealing with men. She looked him up and down. "You know, for a cold-blooded murderer, you're not half bad."

"If I were a cold-blooded murderer, you'd be dead by now."

She laughed. "Whatever you say, killer."

Chip leaned through the Pontiac's open passenger side window and fished Liza's nearly empty pack of Dorals and a book of matches out of her purse. There were just two cigarettes left in the pack, which he believed had to be significant in a weirdly cosmic way. It was symbolic somehow of the strange bond he and Violet were forging. The universe was speaking to him in subtle ways, telling him this was meant to be, that it was the beginning of something wonderful and unique. This struck him as the kind of half-baked "insight" he sometimes had when he was high, but it somehow felt right anyway.

He tore a match from the matchbook and dragged it across the striker, sparking it to life. After lighting up, he passed the last cigarette and matches to Violet. She lit up and they stood there in nearly perfect silence for several minutes. Chip smoked his cigarette down to the filter and stared up at a partially obscured moon sitting behind a veil of wispy, dark clouds.

It was Violet who finally broke the silence. "Can I put my cigarette out on your arm?"

He flicked away the butt of his cigarette and looked at her. "If that's what you want."

She took hold of his arm and stretched it out, turning it to expose the meaty underside of his forearm. Chip cringed, knowing it would be very painful for a few moments. He didn't know why he was allowing her to do this, just knew that it seemed right in that same weird cosmic way.

She smiled sweetly at him.

And then ground the lit end of the cigarette into his previously unmarred flesh. The pain was worse than Chip expected and he cried out as the sickly sweet odor of singed flesh tickled his nostrils. Violet pulled him against her and clutched tightly at his arm, whispering words of comfort as he whimpered in misery. He was suddenly certain there was no worse pain in the world than burn pain.

After a while, the pain began to ebb slightly and he summoned the courage to look at what she'd done to his arm. It was just a little burn, but it was ugly-looking, a bright pink blister puckered at the edges. It needed to be cleaned and swathed in antibiotic gel, but for now all he could do was regard it with a sick fascination. It stunned him that, of his own free will, he'd allowed someone to do this to him. There'd been not even the faintest hint of coercion, just a simple request he'd granted without hesitation.

Violet traced a circle around the burn mark with the tip of a forefinger, taking care to avoid the wound's puckered edge. "There," she said, smiling inscrutably. "There."

Chip frowned. "There...what?"

She drew another invisible circle on his flesh with her forefinger. "That closes the seal."

"I have no idea what you mean."

Violet smiled. "I've bound your soul to mine. From this point forward until the end of time, you belong to me, and I to you. No matter what."

"You're fucking with me again."

She shrugged. "Maybe."

And then she laughed.

Chip thought, *This is one deeply, deeply strange girl. I may be in over my head here.*

She leaned against him and they stood there together a while longer, staring up at the stars and contemplating their own private thoughts.

Then Chip said, "We should probably get out of here."

"Yeah."

20

Chip took the Pontiac back out to the interstate. Rather than heading back to the city, he took the eastbound exit and got on I-24 heading toward Chattanooga. He didn't have a particular destination in mind. It just felt important to put more distance between themselves and the location of the events that had set them down this strange path. Violet either understood his intentions or simply did not care. She closed her eyes shortly after they hit the interstate and fell into a fitful sleep.

Chip kept stealing glances at her as he drove. She slept slumped down in her seat and twisted to one side, with her head resting against the window. Though she was sound asleep, Chip got a clear impression of a troubled mind. Every now and then she would flinch as if in fear of something and several times she uttered the word "no". It was the only word she said as she slept, but the inflection of it varied greatly, ranging from an emotionless monotone to a fragile cry of terror. There was no visible trace of the wanton hellion he'd fucked a short while ago.

He felt pangs of guilt as he watched her, wondering whether the inner distress she was experiencing was a direct result of her hours of captivity in the Pontiac's cramped and dirty trunk, which was the kind of thing that would traumatize just about anyone. In addition, she'd been assaulted and threatened. Chip winced as he remembered the dull clang of the heavy lamp base connecting with her head. That blow had been almost as brutal as the ones he'd dealt to Liza's head, but, so far as he could tell, she was suffering no aftereffects at all.

But maybe she did have a concussion and was just exhibiting her symptoms in a different way. Her behavior was erratic and inappropriate for a kidnapping victim. Wasn't it possible that was a direct result of the physical trauma she'd endured? He wasn't a doctor. He had no idea whether a concussion could cause a drastic personality change. He also knew nothing of Violet's life or what she had been like prior to tonight. Maybe she had always been a weird chick. But, yeah, he certainly couldn't rule out the head injury as an explanation for her odd behavior. And if his hunch was right, it meant he'd taken advantage of a girl not in her right mind for sexual gratification. He'd felt pretty low at various points throughout the night, but this possibility represented his nadir. His self-image could go no lower. And it didn't matter that her behavior had incited and inflamed him. He should have known better, should have had better self-control.

He shook his head.

This was all a bunch of Monday morning quarterbacking. He'd been too in the moment while those things were happening and unable to see past that moment. He'd experienced no small amount of trauma of his own over the course of the night. Which didn't fully excuse his misdeeds, but at least there was some kind of reason he could point to for them.

He'd been driving more than an hour by the time he decided it would be smart to stop somewhere for the night. By now it was past 1:30 a.m. He was tired and needed to rest. His eyes were getting bleary. Soon he'd be struggling to keep them open and his driving would become erratic. Getting stopped by the cops was still right at the top on his list of things he'd rather not have happen.

A green road sign told him he was thirty miles away from Chattanooga, a city of some size. It was where his paternal grandfather lived, though he had no intention of visiting the man. He didn't want to bring any grief into Cecil's life. The old man had enough problems as it was. Even so, the city would be a good place to hole up for a while. Unfortunately, though it was just thirty miles distant, he knew he had to stop sooner. The way his chin kept dipping toward his chest was proof enough of that.

Chip hit the Pontiac's blinker switch and took the next exit. Icons on another road sign indicated there was lodging to be found in the area. He took a right turn off the exit and the first thing he spotted a quarter mile down the road was a convenience store with its lights on. Brighter lights a little farther in the distance marked the likely location of a motel. Deciding it would be a good idea to tend to the still pulsating burn wound first, he pulled in at the convenience store and parked at the lone gas pump on the side facing the street.

After removing the keys from the ignition, he looked at Violet and considered waking her to let her know what he was doing. He changed his mind when he saw that her breathing had become more regular. The bad dreams had passed, it seemed, and she was in a deep state of apparently peaceful sleep. He would have to wake her when they arrived at the motel, but for now there was no harm in allowing her a last few minutes of good rest. In the unlikely event she woke while he was still in the store, she would have no problem figuring out where he was. There would be no reason to panic.

The Pontiac's bashed and scratched driver's side door groaned loudly as Chip opened it and stepped out. He winced at the sound and bent down to peer in at Violet after he eased the door shut. He sighed in relief when he saw she hadn't stirred from her deep slumber.

As Chip approached the store, he scanned the road in both directions and breathed another relieved sigh when he saw no headlights moving through the darkness. He was still carrying evidence of a serious crime, both on his person and inside the car. He hadn't yet had a chance to renew his search for Liza's bloody knife, but he strongly suspected it was in the Pontiac, probably somewhere in the back. Getting rid of that goddamn thing needed to become a top priority, preferably in a way that guaranteed it would never he discovered. He needed to find a significant body of water—a lake, river, whatever—and toss the knife in it. But it was too late an hour and he didn't know the area well enough. Evidence disposal would have to wait for daylight.

An electronic beep sounded when Chip pushed through the entrance into the store. The well-lit store was empty save for himself and the lone clerk behind the counter. The clerk was a skinny, dark-haired girl in her teens. She glanced up from the magazine she was reading and looked at him in the usual bored teenage way. He acknowledged her with a tight nod and a forced smile and she went back to flipping through her magazine.

Chip veered to the right and headed straight to the back, where he pushed through the door to the men's room and locked it behind him. He cringed at the sight of his blood-smeared reflection in the dirty mirror above the sink. After gently probing his still-tender nose to determine once and for all that it was not broken, he pulled a handful of paper towels from a metal dispenser and began the process of cleaning the crusted blood from his face. When he was done, he took a long overdue leak, washed his hands, and walked out of the bathroom.

After a brief walking tour, he spied the little aisle devoted to medicinal items. He pulled packages containing bandages and antibiotic gel off their hooks and carried them to the counter, where he set his items next to the clerk's open magazine. Chip's eyes opened a little wider at the glossy images of two busty and very nude women, who were entwined in a very interesting Sapphic pose.

The clerk looked at him. "Got a problem with that?"

Chip shook his head. "I do not."

"Good."

She rang up his items and read him the total off the register display.

Chip reached for his back pocket, his face twisting in a grimace when he realized he didn't have his wallet on him. It was in the Pontiac's glovebox. Leaving their identification in the car had been another pre-robbery precaution. As such, it had been a perfectly sensible thing to do, but now he was in a bind. The clerk was looking at him a little closer now, a corner of her mouth lifting in a smirk as she began to perceive his predicament. Just as he was about to tell her he needed to run out to the car for a second, he remembered he actually had quite a significant amount of money on him. Paying with robbery money wasn't ideal, but his exhaustion made an extra trip out to the car before he could get on his way a very unattractive proposition.

He opened his jacket and tugged out the envelope of money. He opened the flap, pulled out a hundred-dollar bill, and placed it on the counter.

The clerk was still smirking. She didn't pick up the bill right away. "That's a pretty thick jacket for June. What are you, a biker?"

Chip's gaze flicked out to the parking lot, where the Pontiac was partially obscured by the pump. "Um…"

The clerk laughed. "I saw you pull up in that shitty beater. You're carrying a lot of cash for a guy with a ride like that. Too much, I think. What did you do, rob a bank?"

Chip started feeling a little too hot in his jacket and jeans. The girl was right. The jacket had served a

purpose, but it did not suit the June weather in Tennessee. Plus, it felt like there was no air-conditioning circulating in the little store at all. Sweat stained his shirt at the armpits and made it cling to his back. "Um…"
The clerk's eyes twinkled with amusement. "Maybe you robbed a bank and maybe you didn't. But you did something naughty, that's for sure."
Chip made a face and shook his head. "Are you always this fucking nosy?"
She shrugged. "I mind my own business most of the time."
"Then what the fuck?"
She nodded at the envelope. "That's a lot of money. You did something wrong, who knows, the cops may show up here asking if I saw anything. It happens, you know. I get some of what you're holding, well…maybe my memory gets fuzzy."
Chip placed two more hundred-dollar bills on the counter. "That enough?"
"Little more."
Chip sighed and placed one more bill on the counter. "That's all I'm giving you"
The clerk shifted her stance behind the counter, folding her arms beneath her underdeveloped breasts and standing with all her weight on one leg and a narrow hip cocked outward. It was a pose of resolute defiance. She wasn't smiling anymore, either. "Double it."
"Oh, for fuck's sake."
His exasperation made no impression on her. "Double it and I guarantee I'll forget you were ever here. Don't give me what I want…" She shrugged. "Maybe

my memory gets crystal fucking clear and I call the police to report a suspicious asshole in a leather jacket who came in with blood all over his face and flashed around a bunch of cash."

Chip peeled off five more hundred-dollar bills and added them to the stack of blackmail money. He closed the envelope and returned it to his jacket pocket. "Keep the change," he said, and scooped up the world's costliest ever first aid items.

The clerk's laughter followed him out of the store.

Violet was standing between the pump and the Pontiac's driver's side door. Chip didn't see her until he stepped around the pump and approached the car. Startled by her unexpected appearance, he gasped a little when he saw her. Even more disconcerting was the sight of his 9mm clutched in her hands. He was angry with himself. He was being careless in lots of ways. Some of them were little things, some were more significant, but it all added up to a potentially big problem. He was too tired to think straight. Sleep was imperative, but for a breathless moment he was sure Violet meant to put him to sleep for good.

The gun was pointed toward the ground instead of at him, but that did little to assuage Chip's concerns. He understood right away that Violet had positioned herself behind the pump to conceal her presence, but recognizing that she'd been hiding from the clerk instead of him took a beat or two longer.

Though she couldn't have been awake long, there was no trace of her former sleepiness in her expression.

In its place was a startling fierceness. "I saw you talking to that skinny bitch. Was she flirting with you?"

Chip frowned. "What? No."

Violet stared hard at him and searched his face for signs of deceit. After a moment, her posture relaxed marginally and she said, "I woke up when you took the exit."

"So...you were pretending to be asleep after that?"

"Yes."

"Jesus. You're a really good actress."

"Thank you."

"Why did you do that?"

"To study you, see how you are when you think I'm not watching."

Chip shivered. "Holy shit, that's really kind of creepy."

She grunted. "Look who's talking, robber boy. You were chatting that bitch up for a while. Maybe you were the one doing the flirting."

Chip laughed in a tired, humorless way and ran a hand through his hair. "I assure you I was not flirting with her. Christ, she's a fucking teenager."

Violet's expression got a little darker. "I'm nineteen."

"Are you shitting me?"

"No."

"Well, shit." Chip threw up his hands in abrupt surrender. "You know what? It doesn't matter. Look, here's what really happened..."

She listened as he quickly recounted the tale of impromptu convenience store extortion. As he talked, she directed a series of successively angrier expressions at the store. When he was done, she said, "I'm gonna kill that bitch."

She took a step toward the store.

Chip gripped her by an arm, stopping her in her tracks. "Don't."

Fuming, Violet twisted her arm free of his grip and glared at him. "I want to kill her."

"It's smarter to let it go."

"That's our money. She stole it."

Chip sighed. "And I stole it from someone else. So what? Let it go. Please."

Violet put her hands to the sides of her head and screamed for all she was worth.

"*FUUUUUUUUUUUUUUUUUUUUUCCCCK KKK!*"

Chip stared at her in flabbergasted dismay, his ears ringing for several long seconds after the scream faded. She was making a complete spectacle of herself in a public place. Not the most prudent course of action if you were hoping to avoid the attention of police. Sure, it was very late and the street running by the store was empty of traffic, but even so, it wouldn't take too much more of this kind of behavior to ruin things. Of course, maybe that was the whole point. She had just admitted to faking sleep. And she'd been fucking with him in other ways much of the night. She was a weird chick with inscrutable motives. It could be this was all a twisted bit of fun for her, a protracted exercise in creatively getting back at the more hapless of her two abductors after determining he was no real threat.

She handed him the gun. "Sorry, had to get that out of my system. I know you're right. I'm just tired and not thinking straight."

Chip stared after her as she circled around to the other side of the car and got back inside it. The abrupt acquiescence stunned him nearly as much as the profane—and loud—outburst. It took his brain another few moments to kick back into gear.

Faint pinpoints of light appeared in the distance.

Headlights.

Coming this way.

Chip gave his head a shake to snap himself out the trance.

Violet was smiling when he slid in behind the wheel and set the gun in the tray beneath the radio. She looked calm, as if she didn't have a care in the world.

Maybe she didn't.

Chip started the Pontiac and drove away from the convenience store.

21

The motel a bit farther down the road was just the kind of dirty, out-of-the-way dump Chip was hoping it would be. What the Mongoose Lodge lacked in amenities it more than made up for in the anonymity staying there afforded them. Chip checked in under an assumed name and paid for a night's stay in cash, this time paying with some bills he'd taken from the bulging envelope prior to entering the lobby. The night clerk, a balding and pudgy Latino man in his forties, didn't request identification. The room key was the old-fashioned metal kind rather than the disposable plastic keycards most joints used these days.

The motel's layout was pretty basic. It was a single floor comprised of a couple dozen rooms. Though there was just one other car in the motel's small parking lot, the clerk had given them a room at the far end of the motel. This was totally cool with Chip, who wanted to be as removed from other people as possible. He had a hunch the clerk had somehow sensed this, though he'd barely interacted with the man.

Chip parked the Pontiac with the rear end facing the door to their room. This was so a cop—or anyone else—taking a casual cruise through the parking lot wouldn't be able to read the license plate. It wouldn't help them if someone decided to take a closer look, but Chip figured the odds of that happening were low. That might change if Liza reported the car stolen at some point, but the chances of that happening were also remote. There was DNA evidence in the car that could connect it with a major crime and she wouldn't want to risk the kind of scrutiny that would bring. So he doubted there was an APB out for the Pontiac—unless someone in the neighborhood where he and Liza had performed their imitation of action movie stunt drivers had reported the tag number to police. Given the high-speed nature of the escapade, that also seemed unlikely. Still, it was an easy precaution to take, so why not?

The room was as ratty as expected. The queen-sized bed was tidily made-up, but there were multiple rips in the ancient green carpet, mildew stains on the walls, and cracks of alarming size in the ceiling. But none of this mattered. It was a roof over their heads, a place to crash after a long night.

Violet made a beeline to the bathroom as soon as they were in the room. She slammed the door and in the next instant Chip heard the click of the lock. Door-slamming was usually an indicator of petulance or outright anger, but she had seemed calm prior to entering the room. Chip decided not to worry about it. He couldn't keep up with her changing moods and was too tired to care. Hell, he still couldn't figure out why she wasn't making any effort to get away from him. That alone was a sign of a mind not in good working order.

He shrugged off his jacket, carefully folded it, and set it on the little table by the window. He left the envelope in the jacket. It seemed as good a place as any for it at the moment, given the unsettled state of things. He set his gun on the nightstand next to the bed. The other gun—the one he'd confiscated from Liza prior to leaving her behind—was still in the Pontiac, tucked away beneath a seat. He hoped like hell he wouldn't have cause to shoot anyone else anytime soon. In the event it did happen, he doubted he'd need more than one gun. If he did, he'd be fucked anyway, so whatever.

Chip breathed a sigh of deep weariness as he sat on the edge of the bed and began to pull off his boots. He grunted in relief as they came away from his feet and he waggled his toes a bit after subsequently peeling off the socks. The extent of his exhaustion became even more apparent as he made his bedtime preparations. No pillow had ever looked more inviting than the one on which he was about to lay his head.

Then there was a shriek from the bathroom, the door banged open, and Violet came running back out into the room. She had a look of intense agitation on her face and was thrusting a finger in the direction of the open bathroom door.

"Do something about it!"

Chip just stared at her for a moment. He glanced toward the bathroom. Looked at Violet again. "Do something about...what?"

"The goddamn monster cockroach that tried to crawl up my leg while I was peeing."

Chip groaned and put his face in his hands for a moment before running them through his hair. "You gotta expect that kind of thing in a dump like this. It's no big deal."

Violet picked up the gun and pointed it at his face. "Get off your ass and go kill it."

Chip gave her an incredulous look. "You're not gonna shoot me over a goddamn cockroach."

"The hell I won't."

Chip took the gun out of her hand and set it on the nightstand. "Stop being so dramatic. I'll take care of it."

He got up and walked into the bathroom.

The biggest cockroach he'd ever seen in his life trundled across the tiled floor. The goddamn thing was the Tyrannosaurus Rex of cockroaches. Chip stood in the open doorway and gawked at it for a moment before returning to the nightstand to retrieve the gun. This made Violet laugh. He ignored her and returned to the bathroom, where, after making sure the safety was engaged, he knelt and smashed the pest with the butt of the pistol. Bug guts spurted from its compacted body, making him cringe in disgust. After cleaning up the mess—and washing bug guts off the gun—he walked back out to the main room to gather the first aid items. Violet was standing at the window, holding apart slats in the blind to peer out at the parking lot.

"Anything interesting out there?"

"Not really."

Chip went back to the bathroom, where he cleaned the burn wound at the sink, applied antibiotic gel, and wrapped it up with the bandage. The empty packages went into an overflowing wastebasket by the toilet. Yes, he was definitely getting what he was paying for—a fleabag pit without proper pest control and lackadaisical housekeeping. He wasn't sure what the future held for him after tonight—virtually every aspect of his existence was up in the air—but wherever he landed, it would have to be nicer than this place.

Right?

So he hoped, anyway.

When he walked out of the bathroom again, he was greeted by the sight of Violet lying naked on the bed. Her nude form was, of course, lovely to behold. She was lean and toned, but exquisitely feminine with curves worthy of a centerfold model. If not for the fact that he already felt milked dry after vigorous sexual romps with two different women in the same night, the sight of her exposed body would have frozen his brain.

She smiled. "Ready for your reward?"

"My reward?"

"For coming to my rescue and slaying the dragon. The dragon in this case being a giant-ass, mutant cockroach that probably escaped from some mad scientist's lab."

"I'm not in the mood. Too tired. Sorry."

"Oh, I can fix that."

Chip frowned. "I can't figure you out."

She laughed. "And that's what makes me so interesting."

Chip was in no mood for jokes. "Seriously, what's your deal?"

"What do you mean?"

The playful twist of her smile irritated him. He wasn't normally an irritable person, not any more so than the average guy, anyway, but he was far from his normal self at the moment. "You're not behaving in a rational way. When you tried to shoot me, I understood that. It made sense. Everything since then has not made sense. At all. So I ask you again, one last time, what is your goddamn deal?"

The humor leached out of her expression at last and she regarded him somberly for a while. Then she shifted around on the bed to peel back the covers and slide beneath them, after which she fixed Chip with the same somber expression and said, "Turn out the lights and get in here with me. We'll have the conversation you want." A hint of a smile flickered at the edges of her mouth again. "But take your clothes off first."

Chip wasn't up to arguing with her any further. Besides, lights out sounded good.

Once he was in bed next to her, she curled up against him and draped a leg over his midsection, quite deliberately brushing his cock with her silken-smooth thigh. She put her head on his chest and said, "Ask me anything."

"Why were you at the McKenzies' house? Who are you to them?"

The soft sole of her foot slid over his hip and down the side of his leg. At first Chip assumed she was doing this deliberately to distract him, but when she repeated the motion a few times while making a softly musing sound in her throat, he realized it was just restless, mindless physical motion while she mulled over what to say. The distraction it caused was just a side effect—as was the partial inflation of his cock as her thigh moved against it. He still didn't think he could fuck her again, not yet, but he might be forced to reevaluate that opinion if this continued much longer.

She stopped caressing his leg with her foot and lifted her head off his chest to look at him in the dark. "I guess you could say I sort of…worked for them."

His eyes had adjusted to the dark and he could make out the shape of her face, a fuzzy white oval with a spill of dark hair framing it, but reading her expression was more difficult. He nonetheless detected a hint of something like vulnerability in her voice, sensed there was something profoundly troubling about her relationship with the McKenzies, whatever it had been, and wondered whether that was the reason she wanted to have this talk with the lights off.

Chip thought maybe that was very close to the mark. After some silent minutes elapsed there in the darkness, he realized she needed prompting to continue. "What did you do for them?"

She put her head on his chest again and sighed. "I did stuff for them."

"What kind of stuff?"

"Sex stuff."

He cleared his throat and stared up at the gloom-shrouded ceiling. "Oh."

Her fingers probed his pectoral muscles and she made that musing sound in her throat again. "You're in really good shape, you know that?"

Chip ignored that. "When you say you did 'sex stuff' for them…"

He felt her chin move against his chest as she nodded in apparent affirmation at something running through her head. "I've never talked about it before. It's not the kind of thing you bring up in casual conversation with your friends." She grunted. "Not that I have many friends. I don't really. People think I'm weird."

"Huh."

She did that nodding thing against his chest again. "Don't pretend you haven't noticed. I *am* weird. There's something wrong with me. My head doesn't work right."

"Don't say that."

"Why not? It's just the truth.

For the first time, Chip felt a genuine tenderness toward Violet. He sensed she had been exploited and violated in multiple ways many times long before his and Liza's violent intrusion into her life. "Look, you've said enough. I don't need to know more. It's okay."

She shook her head. "But it's not okay. Not even a little bit. I think I need to tell you everything while my courage is up. I think if I don't, I'll keep it bottled up until I really go crazy and blow my brains out or something."

Chip put a hand to her head, began to lightly stroke her hair. "It's up to you. I'll listen if it's what you really want."

"It is."

"Okay."

She snuggled a little closer against him and let out a shuddery breath. "Okay, so...I used to work for Ken McKenzie. Like, *really* work for him. I worked in administrative support at his office, which basically means I did a lot of boring entry level clerical shit. He flirted with me a lot and I played along with it because, hell, he was the boss. And he was rich. I didn't mind having a rich man pay attention to me. Eventually it turned into more than flirtation and we started an affair. There was a lot of sneaking around. He'd bang me in his office after hours sometimes, but more often we'd hook up at my place or at Ken's secret apartment downtown, the one his wife didn't know about...supposedly. I know it makes me kind of a bad person, but I got off on the idea of screwing another woman's man. Anyway, it turned out the joke was on me, because she knew about it all along. In fact, she was the one who suggested he start hitting on me after she visited the office one day and got a look at me."

Chip frowned. "That's..." He paused, realizing he didn't know what to say to that, could think of no way to adequately express his surprise at this twist in her story. "...different," he wound up finishing, lamely.

She grunted. "About a month into our so-called 'affair' was when Ken first floated the idea of a threesome with his wife. Which, you know, even before all this I was down for the kinky stuff. I'd been with girls before, too. But Madge, that's what he called her, well, the idea of getting with her didn't exactly excite me."

Chip flashed back to his first glimpse of Margaret McKenzie, when she had stepped through that archway just before getting her throat cut by Liza. The memory of all that mottled flab spilling out of that flimsy nightgown made him grimace. "Yeah, I can see that."

Violet's body tensed against him, the memories palpably distressing her. "And I told Ken right away I wasn't really interested, but he kept pushing the idea and when I kept resisting, he hinted I might lose my job if I didn't do what he wanted."

"That motherfucker."

She nodded. "No shit, right? Anyway, I fought back at first, told him if he did that, I'd sue him for sexual harassment. I had voicemail messages from him that would have been pretty good evidence against him in a trial. I figured he'd up the ante with his threats, maybe even really fire me anyway, but that's not what happened."

Chip had a hunch he knew where this was going now, at least to some extent. After all, much of her story mirrored Liza's experience with Ken McKenzie. Only Liza had never gotten freaky with both of the McKenzies. Or had she? She'd never said anything to suggest anything like that had happened, but Chip realized now she wouldn't necessarily have told him. She'd been keeping some other pretty big secrets, after all. And it meant there might have been a reason other than mercenary ruthlessness for the murders.

"He offered you money. Right?"

Violet's hand went from his chest to his shoulder as she clutched at him, seeking comfort. "He offered a *lot* of money, regularly monthly money, more than I could ever hope to make in a job, what with my lack of experience."

Chip clamped down hard on the laugh that wanted to come then. She was just nineteen. No one had much in the way of meaningful workplace experience or skills at that age. Those were things she could have acquired over time, like anyone else. But then the urge to laugh went away as it hit him how cynically Ken McKenzie had used her youth and lack of experience against her. The man had been a real sleazebag. Oddly, or perhaps not so oddly, the more he learned about these manipulative fucks, the less bad he felt about his own—admittedly passive—involvement in their demise.

"So you gave in, I guess."

She sniffled, nodding again. Chip felt moisture on his chest and realized she had been quietly crying for at least a few minutes. "Yeah, I did. And once they had their hooks in me, there was nothing I could do to get myself out of it. The McKenzies became obsessed with me. Ken pressured me into quitting my job and moving in with them and I did that, too. By then it was easier to just go along with whatever they wanted. They treated me like a slave, made me do all kinds of disgusting, perverted shit. And Madge was way worse than Ken that way. That woman was a fucking monster."

Chip sighed and shook his head. "Damn, just...damn."

"I know. It was fucked up. I don't even care that they're dead, you know. If anybody ever had it coming, it was them. But when I came downstairs last night and saw them that way...well, it just scared the shit out of me."

Chip grunted. "It scared the shit out of me, too."

"So it was really Liza who did all that?"

"Yeah, it was really her."

"And you really didn't know she planned to kill them?"

"I really didn't know. Swear to fucking God."

She put her face closer to his and he felt a soft exhalation of warm breath against his skin. "I believe you." She kissed him lightly on the mouth, nibbled gently at his bottom lip. "You're a good guy, I think."

He laughed. "I'm a thief. And a loser."

She kissed his chin. "You saved me. Maybe you didn't want to at first because you were scared, but you did. That means you're good. And the opposite of a loser. I don't care about the rest of it."

There were some omissions, things she didn't know, but what she said was close enough to the real truth about him. Correcting her on the rest of it would serve no good purpose. She shifted against him, dragging her thigh over his cock yet again. This time his physical response was more lively. She climbed atop him and they made the ancient bedsprings squeak for a while. It was less frenzied than the first time and in the end his utter physical and mental exhaustion caused him to slowly wilt inside her. He stayed hard long enough for Violet to ride him to gasping orgasm one more time, though, and that was good enough. Afterward they held each other some more, in total silence this time, and soon settled into a sleep far more peaceful than either had anticipated.

22

  Violet was gone when Chip woke up later that morning. His initial reaction to her absence was subdued. Bright sunlight blazed through the plastic slats of the window blind as his eyes fluttered open, illuminating the empty part of the mattress where she had slept with him through those last hours of pre-dawn darkness. Figuring she was in the bathroom, he closed his eyes and fell back into a light doze. When he stirred awake again, the sunlight was even brighter and he could feel the warmth of it on his bare back.
  Violet was still gone.
  Though still not really alarmed, he became more alert as awareness of her absence became more pronounced. He didn't know how long she'd been gone and had only a dim notion of how long he'd dozed this time. He thought it might have been only a few minutes, but it could have been as long as a half hour. His head felt fuzzier than it should, almost the way it did after a night of drinking.
  Chip rolled onto his back with a groan and looked at the bedside clock. He frowned when he realized he'd slept almost the entire morning. Noon was just twenty minutes away. The sense of something being off began to dawn after a few more moments of consciousness. He

was still groggy and it took him a few additional moments to pinpoint the nature of that something wrong. He squinted hard at the nightstand as his powers of perception slowly began to sharpen.

    On the nightstand was the lamp.
    An old phone with a rotary dial.
    And the clock.
    But the gun was gone.
    Chip's eyes snapped wide open.
    Oh, shit!
    He threw the covers back and swung his legs over the side of the bed. His gaze went immediately to the table. There was no sign of his jacket. Chip's heart started pounding faster and faster. His mouth was dry and his throat felt tight. Panic was setting in.
    The money! Oh shit, where's the money!?
    He had not gone through all that hell last night just to lose the goddamn money. People had died because of that money. His whole life had been upended in pursuit of it. No way could that whole wild night of chaos, death, and destruction have been for nothing. The prospect of it filled him with a gut-wrenching, paralyzing sense of anguish. But the paralysis was soon overwhelmed by anger, directed both at himself and at Violet for having duped him. He couldn't believe he'd fallen for her preposterous sob story. In the bright light of day, he understood clearly what his exhausted and overtaxed mind had been blind to last night. She had played him for a sap, taking advantage of his guileless nature by plying him with her luscious body and manipulating him emotionally with her tale of woe.

Thoughts foreign to anything he'd ever entertained flitted through his head. These were fevered imaginings of blood and vengeance. He pictured himself tracking Violet down and taking the money back. It unfolded like scenes from a movie. Here he was speeding down a ribbon of black highway, his face grim behind the wheel, suitably dramatic music pounding in the background as he followed a trail of clues leading to his quarry. Then came the interrogation scenes, in which he intimidated or beat the information he needed out of Violet's associates. And then the big finale, the ultimate showdown with the devious villainess who'd taken everything from him. They fought like foes in an action movie. She had an inexplicable arsenal of devastating martial arts moves, which she used to knock the living shit out of him. Yet somehow he was still standing at the end, bruised and bloodied but not defeated. Like any overconfident villain, she made the mistake of underestimating the hero. He rallied, took advantage of her sudden sloppiness, and wound up beating her to death with his bare hands. After which he retrieved the stolen cash and staggered off into the sunset with triumphant music bleeding into the closing credits.

    This all went through his mind in the space of maybe a minute. He understood how ridiculous his mind-movie was, but it had a galvanizing effect anyway. Maybe he didn't have it in him to go all Jason Statham on Violet, but that didn't mean he couldn't go after her and try to get the money back. It would just happen with probably a lot less ass-kicking and maybe not so much in the way of conveniently cued soundtrack music.

Chip got up and walked over to the window. A peek through blind slats confirmed another of his fears. The Pontiac was also gone. So she had taken his money, his transportation, and his means to defend himself. He was working at a disadvantage on multiple levels, but there were still some moves he could make. He wasn't far from Chattanooga. He could call his grandfather. The old man could come pick him up and take him back to his place, where he could stay long enough to begin devising a plan. Chip supposed he would have to swallow his pride and borrow a bit of money from him. Cecil could spare a little. He wasn't rich, but he wasn't indigent, either. And with some money in his pocket, Chip would suddenly have a few more options at his disposal.

His cell phone was gone along with his jacket, but he could use the room phone to call Cecil. He turned away from the window intending to do just that, but that was when he realized still more things were missing. The clothes he'd left in a pile on the floor before climbing into bed with Violet had also disappeared.

Chip put a hand to his forehead and chuckled in amused dismay.

Sweet Jesus, but that bitch was thorough!

He pictured her quickly and quietly scuttling about the room, meticulously gathering all his things while simultaneously keeping a watchful eye on him for signs of imminent wakefulness. Shaking his head, he wondered how long she'd been gone. Had she waited until first light? Or had she gone to work as soon as she knew he was fast asleep? His gut told him it was the latter. Having hatched the plan, she wouldn't have wanted to waste any time putting it into action. And she would have taken every step she could to slow him down when he woke up and realized what had happened, thus the removal of his clothes. Her reasoning on this count was easy to understand. He couldn't very well go roaming around outside naked, could he? That kind of thing could get him picked up by the cops in a hurry and she knew he didn't want that to happen. Well, it was a risk he could take if he got desperate enough, but he hoped it wouldn't come to that.

Chip sat on the edge of the bed and lifted the old phone's receiver off the cradle. He already had a finger in the rotary dial when he put the receiver to his ear and realized there was no dial tone. Frowning, he punched the hook in a few times in hopes of triggering a tone. Being relatively young at almost thirty, he had little to no experience with phones of this type, but he'd seen this trick work in old movies.

It wasn't working now.

He reached behind the phone and pulled at the cord. There was no tug of resistance and in a moment it was apparent why—the line had been cut

"For fuck's sake."

Chip flipped the cord away in disgust and set the useless receiver back on the cradle.

Well, she'd certainly covered all the bases, he had to give her that.

Chip put his face in his hands and just sat there for many long moments, now at a complete loss as to what to do next. He envisioned a surreal future of permanent confinement to this sleazy, roach-infested pit of a room. He would be like a character in a Kafka novel. Not that he'd ever actually read a Kafka novel. But he'd heard the word "surreal" bandied about when intellectuals—or poseurs—talked about them. Also, he thought there was something to do with a cockroach in one of them, so it kind of fit his situation. He further imagined describing this phase of his life to enthralled listeners at a later point, when all this insanity was behind him. He would say, "Yeah, it was a totally Kafkaesque kind of deal." And then everyone would nod sagely and not say anything because no one would know what the hell he meant by that, only that it was very deep and existential and all that kind of shit.

But of course that was all bullshit because before long the motel manager would come around to either kick him out or demand payment for another night. Sans clothes and money, that promised to be a really interesting conversation. Chip tried hard to imagine a way he might adequately explain his situation and failed. Even with some of the more questionable bits glossed over, it was apt to sound deranged. The manager would call the cops and then the jig would be up. He doubted he was a person of interest yet in the McKenzie murders, but any halfway competent cop would immediately suspect he'd been up to no good.

Maybe they couldn't arrest him for anything, at least not yet, but they wouldn't be able to help him much either. Reporting the Pontiac as stolen remained a very chancy proposition. There were a lot of nasty things he could say about Violet now that she'd ditched him, but she wasn't dumb. She wouldn't want to spend a lot of time in a tainted vehicle. With the money she had, she could buy another cheap beater or a bus ticket to somewhere far away. But on the off-chance the cops did nab her for stealing the car, she would undoubtedly start spilling a lot of information Chip wouldn't want them to know.

So, yeah, fuck that noise.

Chip sat on the edge of the bed mentally spinning his wheels a while longer. His total inability to do *anything* about his situation was beyond frustrating. Eventually he realized he had to take a piss and got up to go to the bathroom.

Which was when he got his biggest shock yet.

23

Violet was dead in the bathtub with her throat cut ear to ear. Chip stood there frozen for a long moment. His head was empty of all thought during that time, not because he was numb from shock but because his mind was incapable of processing what he was seeing. Of all the things he'd imagined might have happened to Violet, this had not been among them. If he'd turned the possibilities over in his head for a million years, he wouldn't have thought of it for the simple reason that he couldn't begin to conceive of how it had happened.

Some assassin had come into their room during the night and had done this to her without ever waking him. The level of stealth required to accomplish the deed boggled the mind. It was the sort of thing he associated with ninjas, secret agents, and a host of other exotic nefarious characters from movies. For the most part, Chip had lived an unassuming life on the margins of society. He knew no ninjas or secret agents, was pretty sure they moved in completely different social circles. And anyway, he wasn't worthy of the attention of anyone like that, regardless of anything he'd done.

He sucked in an abrupt big breath as tears stung his eyes. The tears signaled the end of that frozen moment. The reality of what he was seeing hit him hard.

The shame he felt as he recalled his violent fantasies about catching up to Violet staggered him, forced him to brace his hands on the doorjamb to remain upright.

The poor girl had died messily. The cut to her throat was deep. Her attacker had almost taken her head off. There was a lot of blood in the tub, as well as some arterial spatter on the floor tiles. Someone strong had manhandled her into the tub and held her down and then killed her, all while making a minimal amount of noise. He still couldn't comprehend it. She had gone to bed nude and had died that way, which made Chip wonder whether the assault had been sexual in nature. He had no way of determining that, but it seemed a logical conclusion. She was—had been—a beautiful girl. It was possible a predator staying in another room at the motel had seen them arriving and had made an impulsive decision to go after her.

Chip retreated from the bathroom and ran across the room to peer out the window again. He remembered there had been just one other car parked in front of one of the other rooms when they arrived. At the time he'd been too tired to take note of make and model, but his memory supplied him with a vague image of a blue four-door sedan. He had an even vaguer impression of the mystery car being old, though not as old as the Pontiac, a tan-colored 70's relic.

He thumped a fist against the wall. "Shit!"

The blue sedan was gone. The only other car was parked on the far side of the lot, over by the lobby/office area. It had to belong to whoever was on duty at the motel today. He stepped away from the window and marched back and forth across the room a few times, gnawing at a knuckle on a clenched fist as he tried hard to think of something—anything—he could do. He knocked over a chair and screeched again in frustration. The situation looked hopeless from every angle. Violet's killer was somewhere loose out there and there was nothing at all he could do about it. He couldn't even call the cops to report her murder.

The cops.

Chip swallowed with some difficulty and abruptly stopped pacing.

Oh, man. Oh, shit. Oh, shit, shit, shit...

The one thing he'd had working in his favor until now was that there wasn't much in the way of physical evidence to connect him to anything serious. That was no longer the case. There was a dead girl in the room with him and her death was something he couldn't hope to conceal very long. There was a ton of DNA evidence present. His fingerprints. Hair fibers on the mattress. And, hell, forget the room, there was a ton of his DNA *on*—and inside—Violet's body. Anyone investigating the scene would come to an inescapable conclusion—*he* had killed her. As he considered this, it hit him how wholly unbelievable the police would find his story. No one would buy that he'd slept through the whole thing and he wouldn't be able to blame them because he didn't understand it himself.

Chip wandered back over to the bathroom and peeked in at Violet again. He didn't want to look at what had been done to her, but he felt like he had to force himself to do it to have any hope of figuring a way out of this seemingly impossible mess. This time, thinking he would get right up to the tub and kneel down for the closest possible forensic examination, he took a step into the bathroom and winced at the feel of coagulated blood spatter beneath his feet.

He took one more step into the room and something from the corner of his eye snagged his attention. Though he hadn't seen it yet, a sense of deep foreboding overcame him. With great reluctance, he turned toward the mirror above the sink.

Chip felt suddenly deflated.

"Shit."

A single word had been scrawled across the mirror in Violet's blood: *CHEATER.*

He shook his head. "Goddammit."

With that one word, so much became instantly clear. Violet had not met her demise at the hands of some random sex predator. He belatedly realized he should have guessed that already based on the theft of his things and the money.

Liza.

He didn't know how she'd managed to track him down so quickly—hell, she should be in a fucking hospital right now—but there was no question in his mind that she had somehow done it. She had always claimed she was so much smarter than he was and, well, here was the ultimate proof. The more he turned the notion over in his head, the more it all made sense. This was personal. The bloody message on the mirror confirmed that. But the truth should have been clear even without it. A random predator wouldn't have killed Violet and left him alive.

So, okay, Liza had tracked him down.

And she had somehow gotten into their room, at which point she had seen him asleep in bed with Violet. The sight of their nude forms entwined would have inflamed her fury. Liza was a cold-hearted bitch in many ways, but she loved Chip. Or at least she thought of him as belonging exclusively to her. He had a hunch he knew how she had seen things. This other woman had enticed him into running away with her and the money. The truth wasn't exactly like that. He'd had no plan, no thought of what might come next. He'd spent the whole night reacting and nothing else. But Liza wouldn't have known these things. In her eyes, he was guilty of betrayal and so she'd killed Violet as an object lesson. He still didn't get how she'd done that without waking him, but it wasn't worth getting hung up on that point. She had done it, no question. The throat-cutting certainly fit her MO.

And as for why she had left him alive in the wake of his betrayal?

Well, that was pretty obvious, too.

This was a frame-up. It was why she'd given him no way out of the room. Chip couldn't help but shake his head in admiration at the audacity of it all. He walked back out to the room and sat on the bed to await the sound of sirens.

24

An hour passed and nothing happened. Chip was beginning to think Liza had left him entirely to his own devices, which made little to no sense. Why go to the trouble of setting him up and then fail to send the cops after him? The longer he sat there and waited for doom to come crashing down on him in the form of the police arriving en masse to take him down and take him away, the less sense a lot of his theory made. That it was a set-up still felt right. That part was obviously the largest part of what had happened. But nothing else fit.

There were a lot of little things that didn't quite add up, but one factor loomed larger than all the others—the fact that he was still alive. Liza had frequently professed her deep love for him. She had done it even after he'd knocked her on the head and led her on a mad chase through one of the seedier parts of Nashville. So clearly she was willing to forgive a lot where he was concerned. But Chip couldn't see Liza allowing her emotions to get in the way of self-interest. Her number one concern would have been how the setup scheme impacted her. And there just wasn't any upside to leaving him alive, not when he had so much he could tell the police about her role in the deaths of the McKenzies and her activities in support of her brother's "research."

Chip tried hard to think of an alternate explanation for what had happened while he was asleep, but he came up empty. Despite the holes in his original theory, Liza killing Violet and framing him for the murder was the only thing that accounted for the central facts of the situation. Somewhere out there was information he just didn't have, some essential missing element on which it all hinged—and which would explain why he was still alive and not yet in police custody. If he could find out what that mystery element was, the rest of it would fall into place.

But that couldn't happen if he continued to sit here and do nothing. The longer he did that, the greater the chance of discovery by police or motel staff became. Like it or not, the time had come to take some kind of risk, to do something bold. At first he came up empty on that front, too, but then he had a flash of inspiration.

He rolled off the bed and went back to the bathroom. This time he avoided looking directly at Violet's body. He'd had a good bit of time to stew over the fact that she hadn't run out on him, after all. He didn't know what ultimately would have happened between them. Maybe nothing. Maybe something. It was all so fresh and unsettled, despite the intimacies they'd shared. He kept thinking about the "seal" she'd drawn around his burn wound with her fingertip and what she'd said about that, how they would then be bound to each other forever. She'd been a weird girl, no doubt, but she hadn't deserved to die. Chip wasn't a believer in love at first sight. That was fairy tale garbage, soap opera crap that had nothing to do with the real world. But despite the strange and brief nature of their time together, he'd begun to feel something for her. He wished like hell there'd been a chance to find out what that something could have become.

A single thin towel hung from a rack on the wall. Chip grabbed the towel and wrapped it around his waist as he walked out of the bathroom. Once he was satisfied the towel was securely in place, he took a last peek out the window by the front door and left the room.

25

Chip walked at a brisk pace down the sidewalk toward the lobby. He was a self-conscious guy in a lot of ways, which was yet another aspect of his personality Liza had never been shy about exploiting. Strutting around outdoors with nothing but a wisp of a towel to conceal his private parts was not the kind of thing he would ever normally do. Sure, there was more of him covered up than there would be if he was poolside in his swimming trunks, but context mattered. He *wasn't* poolside and, anyway, this dump didn't have a pool. Anyone who happened to observe him would know this and wouldn't be able to help staring. And knowing he had a decent body made the prospect of being stared at while towel-clad no less unsettling—in some ways, it made it worse.

Luckily for him, the motel appeared completely deserted. The red Hyundai over by the lobby remained the only vehicle in sight. Chip was grateful for this for a number of reasons, not the least of which was his modesty.

Another pudgy Latino man sat behind the desk when Chip pushed through the front door and entered the lobby. That he was not the same pudgy Latino man who'd been on duty when he and Violet checked in during the wee hours was immediately apparent. Though there was an obvious family resemblance, this man was older, fatter, and had less hair. He also wore thick-lensed glasses in big black frames. The glasses made his eyes look too big, like the eyes of an alien or monster from some other dimension, like a thing in a bad human disguise. Just looking at the guy gave Chip the shivers. To be fair, though, his nerves were on edge and he was inclined to see sinister implications in just about everything.

The guy looked up from the folded-over section of newspaper he'd been reading and frowned at Chip's unorthodox attire. "Problem, sir?"

Chip couldn't help laughing at that.

"You could say that, yeah."

"How may I help?"

Chip braced his hands on the edge of the desk and leaned over it a little to scrutinize the area behind it. There was a corkboard on the wall behind the clerk with keys hanging from neat rows of pegs. Only one peg was missing a key. So Chip was currently the only guest checked-in at the Mongoose Lodge. That was a good thing to know. It meant that if things went south here, he'd at least have some slim chance of getting away undetected. He had a vague notion of overpowering this guy and maybe stowing him in the back. He could tie the dude up, turn on the "No Vacancy" sign (though that would be kind of a laugh given the parking lot's emptiness), and drive that red Hyundai back to Nashville.

But he was hoping it wouldn't come to that.

"Well, I've got sort of a situation and I was hoping I could use your phone." He nodded at the rotary phone on the desk. Next to it was a tattered copy of the Yellow Pages, a thick one that was probably long out-of-date. Everything about this place made him feel like he'd stepped through a portal in time back to the goddamn 1940's. Except that Latino families probably didn't own shithole motels in Tennessee back then. "Would that be okay?"

The old man gave a lazy shrug of his shoulders, causing his sizable man-boobs to strain against the fabric of his striped polo shirt, which was at least a size too small for him. "Why would you not use your room phone?"

"It's out of order."

The man's bushy eyebrows drew together, causing the deep furrows in his forehead to become more pronounced thus slightly heightening the impression of a creature hiding behind a human mask. "That is very strange. Is the jack plugged into the wall?"

"It is, yes."

But the cord's been cut, so let's move on, please...

"Very strange."

Chip nodded.

Yep, you already said that.

He was trying hard to hide his impatience and deep anxiety, but it was difficult.

The old man sighed. "Would this call be long-distance?"

Chip hesitated. He was of a generation that by and large only used cell phones. He wasn't totally sure how "long-distance" worked. Was it long distance if the call was to someone in the same state? He just didn't know. His impulse was to lie, but he was unconvinced it would help him. "It's in the 615 area code."

"That is long-distance."

"Well, shit."

The old man smiled in commiseration. "Might your 'situation' have anything to do with the party last night?"

Chip frowned. "The what?"

"You are in room 1024, correct?"

Chip thought about it. "Uh...yeah. I think so. But what's this about a party? We went to bed as soon as we checked in." He regretted the reference to a companion the moment it slipped his lips. There had been no need for it. Violet had stayed in the car while he paid for the room. As far as these people knew, he'd been traveling alone. Well, so much for that. "There was another car here when we checked in, a blue sedan. It was parked outside a room a few doors down from us. I don't remember any noise, though. If they were having a party, we didn't have anything to do with it."

The old man shook his head. "I wasn't here. I can only tell you what my nephew told me. He was working this morning when you arrived."

"And he told you room 1024 was having a party?"

The old man nodded. "He said there was a lot of noise. Music, loud laughter, that sort of thing. In fact, there was so much noise the other guest left because of it."

"Oh."

Though the old man seemed good-natured in general, his expression turned grave, which had the effect of making his eyes look even freakier behind the absurdly thick lenses. "Oh, yes. He demanded and received a refund. Your party cost us money, Mr. Delacroix." He waved a liver-spotted hand at the door behind Chip to indicate, presumably, the barren parking lot. "As you can see, we're not busy this time of year. Or ever these days, truth be told. Every dollar earned is precious."

Chip stared blankly at the old Latino for a moment. His confusion stemmed from being called "Mr. Delacroix", the alias he'd used when signing the register. He had no idea why he'd used that name. It'd just popped into his head. "Right. Well...I'm real sorry about that, Mr..."

"Hernandez."

Chip smiled. "Mr. Hernandez. Listen, I'm real sorry about any hardship I might have caused and I'd like a chance to make it up to you. I swear on my mother's grave, I have no memory of this party, but I guess I got too drunk or something. I'll make up the money you lost, even give you a little extra. But to do that I'll need to use your phone. So...can I do that? I'll pay for the call, too, of course."

Hernandez scratched his chin and gave Chip an appraising look before replying. "You seem in some distress, Mr. Delacroix."

Chip laughed. "You could say that, yeah. That girl I was with last night? Well, turns out I made a bad choice when I picked her up at that bar." Chip was winging it now. He'd become adept at creating passably believable fictions on the fly during his two years with Liza, who was an absolute master of the art. "She was a hot little number and I guess I let my animal urges get the better of me. She must have roofied me last night. Sure, fuck, I bet that's what happened. It explains why I can't remember a thing."

Hernandez frowned. "Roofied?"

"It's slang. She drugged me, is what I'm saying. This girl must have slipped me a roofie-laced drink. Jesus." Chip shook his head ruefully. "That explains everything."

Though he was winging it, Chip had the unsettling sense of having stumbled upon a piece of the real truth. *Something* explained how Violet had been viciously murdered while he slept through the whole thing and being drugged made as much sense as anything else. It even went a ways toward plugging the holes in the theory of Liza perpetrating Violet's murder as a revenge killing for him being unfaithful. Maybe she'd thought it would wipe his memory of the entire night instead of just the grisly details of Violet's death. That had to be it. It made his continued presence among the living much less inexplicable.

But Liza had miscalculated. He had a lot of complicated emotions where she was involved. He'd loved and feared her and, yes, on occasion some of the things she did had upset him. But he'd never felt anything like the murderous rage he was feeling now. He wanted to kill her.

Hernandez became more wary of Chip at this visible darkening of his mood. He edged away from him a little, moving toward the other end of the desk. His gaze flicked to something beneath the desk before shifting back to Chip. He licked his lips and smiled in a forced way. Chip had the impression he was trying not to seem nervous.

He was a really terrible actor.

Chip held up his hands and took a small step backward. "Hey, chill, okay?" He infused his voice with as much sincerity as he could muster, knowing he needed to convince the man of his essential harmlessness within about ten seconds or he was fucked. "No need to go for your gun or whatever you've got stashed back there. I'm just a guy in an unfortunate situation I'm trying to work my way out of. You've got nothing to fear from me. My car, my money, and my clothes are all gone because that bitch drugged and robbed me. That's why I'm standing here in your lobby wearing a towel like an idiot. If I could just use your phone, I can fix all this. I can get a friend of mine to bring me some clothes and money. And then *you'll* get money, enough to cover the inconvenience I've caused you and then some. You'd like that, wouldn't you?"

His words appeared to placate Hernandez, whose smile was warmer now and devoid of its former falseness. "Forgive me, Mr. Delacroix, but I've had incidents with thieves before. It's a hazard of working alone. You may place your call. I can also offer a temporary solution to one of your problems. I have a lost-and-found box of assorted clothing items left behind by guests. You may sort through them to see if any might fit you."

Chip smiled in relief. That was one potential crisis averted. Too bad the rest of it couldn't be so easily fixed. "Thank you."

Hernandez pushed the phone toward him. "You must first dial a 9."

Chip put the receiver to his ear and dialed Liza's cell number. The line rang twice before being answered by an unfamiliar male voice. "Who is this?"

Chip didn't say anything. He was too flabbergasted by the unexpected voice in his ear. The person on the other end was a stranger to him—he was sure of it—but there was a brusque quality to his tone that was disquieting. Hearing it made his heart start racing again.

"Hello?"

Chip cleared his throat. "Um…sorry, I must have dialed the wrong number."

"Did you call--"

The brusque male voice recited Liza's number.

Chip's tongue felt too thick in his mouth. For a moment, he couldn't breathe much less force out a reply. He was finally able to spit out some words when the unfriendly voice prompted him again. "Yes, I'm calling for Liza. She's a…friend. Is something wrong?"

The man on the other end grunted. "Your name, please."

"Mark Delacroix."

"Mr. Delacroix, my name is Vance Morgan. I'm a detective with the Metro-Nashville police department."

Chip's grip tightened around the receiver.
Oh, motherfucking shitballs.

26

The conversation with the detective was short but informative. Liza was in a coma at Baptist Hospital in Nashville after enduring "blunt-force trauma" caused by an altercation with an unknown assailant, resulting in a nearly fatal brain hemorrhage. She had been there all morning. Other than these essential facts, the detective could not provide additional details regarding her condition. It was not necessary to feign the shock Chip felt upon hearing this news. The detective wanted to know if he had any information about Liza's activities during the night. Chip denied any such knowledge and came across as so distraught by the news about Liza that Morgan opted not to press the issue. He informed Chip he could contact the hospital for more information and then ended the call.

Hernandez gave him a sympathetic look. "Bad news, Mr. Delacroix?"

"You could say that."

Chip felt light-headed. The news about Liza flipped everything upside down and turned it inside-out. It stunned him to learn he'd hurt her bad enough to endanger her life. And any sense of having a handle on what had happened while he was asleep had now been completely obliterated. Liza couldn't have killed Violet because she'd been fighting for her own life all that time. His thoughts briefly turned to Dwayne, but he dismissed the possibility almost right away. Scary though he was, that guy was out of commission, no doubt about it. And the idea of the guy tracking him down to this place on his own was ludicrous.

So...who had killed Violet?

Hernandez looked concerned. "Do you need to sit down, Mr. Delacroix? Can I get you a glass of water?"

"A glass of water? What the fuck for?"

Hernandez shrugged. "I'm just trying to help."

Chip grimaced. "I know. I'm sorry for snapping. I just got some really bad news and I'm having a hard time dealing with it."

"Your friend cannot come?"

Chip shook his head. "Not that friend. But don't worry, I can call someone else." The only person he could feasibly call was his grandfather, but he felt a lot less inclined to do that in light of how things had changed. Hernandez didn't need to know that, though. "But before I do that, is there anything else you can tell me about this party last night? Did your nephew get a look at anyone going in or out of my room?"

Chip didn't expect an answer to this. Clearly the powers-that-be in the universe were conspiring to make every aspect of the mystery engulfing his life impossible to figure out. But Hernandez surprised him. "He saw two others. He paid attention because of the ruckus. He said these others went in and out of your room several times."

"Did he give you a description?"

Hernandez nodded. "The young man was skinny and had blond hair. The girl was skinny and had dark hair. My nephew thought she might be a boy at first because she wasn't..." Here Hernandez paused and used his hands to describe an hourglass figure in the air. "But this girl yelled at the young man. Hector, that's my nephew, said it was the voice of a female. And her hair was long."

Chip nodded as Hernandez told him these things. As he listened, much of the tension gripping him dissipated. There was much he didn't know, of course, but he thought he knew the identity of that girl. How could he forget someone who'd extorted a grand out of him?

"I'm real sorry about this, Mr. Hernandez."

Hernandez frowned. "Sorry about what, Mr. Delacroix?"

Chip seized the front of the man's polo shirt and pulled him against the desk. The old man's hand drifted toward whatever was concealed beneath the desk, but he couldn't quite reach it and his fingers twitched spastically as he strained for it. Chip grabbed the heavy base of the old rotary phone and slammed it against the side of Hernandez's head as hard as he could. The blow opened a gash above his ear and dark blood spurted from the wound. Hernandez squawked in pain and fell against the desk. He was injured but not unconscious, staring at Chip from behind those thick lenses with those horribly big, googly eyes of his. Chip smashed the phone against the man's head three more times and then relinquished his grip on him. The old man flopped backward and landed with a hard thump on the floor.

Chip slammed the blood-spattered phone down on the desk with a cry that was equal parts helpless rage and despair. Hurting an old man who'd only done his best to help him was a really low thing to do. It was the kind of thing only the worst criminal scumbags did. He couldn't hide from the truth any longer—he was now a full-fledged member of the ancient order of lowlifes and criminal cretins, a scumbag with a capital S.

And yet, what else could he have done?

He was in the worst kind of impossible bind. Some other scumbags had targeted him and backed him into a corner and the only way out was through violent, unhesitating action. Anything else meant surrender. It meant going to jail, maybe on death row if the state convicted him for Violet's murder. He'd wavered on the verge of surrender and acceptance of his situation earlier, but that was before he possessed the information he had now. He had a line on his money and the people who'd set him up. The chances of catching up to them and retrieving what was his were slim, but as long as the opportunity existed at all he had to pursue it with unflinching ruthlessness.

Chip climbed over the desk and dropped down to the floor on the other side. He knelt next to Hernandez and took his pulse. At first there was nothing and Chip gritted his teeth against the scream that wanted to come. His course was set and there was no turning back now, but the possible fact of the man's death tore at him. Then he felt it, a pulse, low and faint, but definitely there.

Chip heaved a breath.
Oh, thank God.
There was a door behind him. Chip opened it and peered through it into a small office. Inside it were a couple of tall filing cabinets and a small, flat-topped desk. There were some framed pictures of family members on the desk. Hernandez's nephew was smiling broadly in one of them and had an arm around a middle-aged white woman, who was maybe his wife. Another picture showed the elder Hernandez in a similar pose with a Latino woman his approximate age. Chip wished he hadn't seen the goddamn pictures. The personalizing of Hernandez made what he was doing even harder. This was a family man who had lots of people who cared about him.
Shit.
Chip dragged Hernandez into the little office and closed the door. He didn't want anyone who might walk in catching a glimpse of what he was doing. After all, most people with at least a few reasonably functional brain cells were apt to find the sight of a half-naked man manhandling a bloody body suspicious. Of course, there were other things that were likely to set off alarms in the mind of an interloper—the blood spatter on the reception desk, for instance—but he could worry about that once he got the old man squared away.

He sat in the chair behind the desk and started opening drawers. There was nothing of much use in the top and middle drawers, but he sighed in relief when he spied a very useful item at the back of the larger, junk-cluttered bottom drawer—a fresh, unused roll of silver duct tape. Chip grabbed it and set to work binding the old man. Duct tape alone wasn't ideal for restraining a guy, but it should keep him out of commission until he could get gone from this place. He used liberal amounts of tape, wrapping it around Hernandez's wrists and ankles dozens of times, sometimes winding it between the limbs in alternating crisscross patterns, which he hoped would make getting loose harder. Once he was satisfied with that part of it, he sealed the man's mouth with another layer of tape. Chip hated to do it. It would make breathing harder, might even make the difference between life and death, but he had no choice. He couldn't have the guy screaming for help if he regained consciousness.

Once this task was done, he opened the door a crack and peered out at the lobby, which was still empty. From his vantage point, he could see the underside of the reception desk. There were some shelves to the left and an open space to the right. Propped in a corner of the open space was a golf club. It was the kind with a heavy, thick clubhead. Chip was pretty sure it was called a driver or a wood. The club was what Hernandez had been reaching for under the desk, which was kind of disappointing. He'd been hoping for a gun, which would have equalized the situation when he went hunting for his money. But it was better than nothing. He'd take it with him when he left.

Also in the open space was an unsealed cardboard box, which had to contain the assortment of lost-and-found clothes Hernandez had mentioned. Chip opened the door wider, stepped out of the office, and eased the door shut behind him. He crept over to the desk, taking care not to slip in the little puddle of blood behind it. He pulled the box out and began to sort through the irregular assortment of unwanted clothes. The clothes had been laundered and neatly folded, but that was the best Chip could say about the collection. All in all, they were the kind of items you couldn't blame a person for leaving behind, including plain white T's and various pieces of underwear bearing stains even the strongest detergent couldn't completely erase. If *he* were running this place, the fucking underwear would have gone in the garbage. The remaining items were a small selection of things a person with low standards might actually wear out in public. At the moment, Chip's standards were quite low indeed, so that was okay. The one pair of men's jeans was too small. He wound up pulling on a pair of grey sweatpants with a couple of small holes in the butt area. A plain white T in his size went on over his head. It was a relief to be clothed again, however poorly. At the bottom of the box was the sole piece of available footwear—a pair of pink women's flip-flops with shiny plastic "diamonds" on the Y-shaped strap. Feeling like the world's biggest ass, Chip put the flip-flops on.

    A check of the shelves beneath the desk turned up Hernandez's keys, which he dropped in a hip pocket. After wiping the blood off the counter with the discarded towel, he set about wiping down any other surface he might have touched. He went back into the office and did the same, handling the doorknob on his way back out with the towel. Getting rid of all DNA evidence tying him to this probably wasn't possible, but Chip felt compelled to at least try. When he was done, he went to the lobby door and peered out at the lot. Hernandez's red Hyundai was still the only car in sight. He might yet have time to back the car up to room 1024 and load everything he could—Violet's body and the bed sheets they'd slept on during the night—into the trunk for later disposal.

Still using the towel to avoid leaving fingerprints, he gripped the doorknob, turned it, and began to pull open the door. He froze when a glint of sunlight hit the windshield of a car approaching from the direction of the interstate junction. He held his breath and inwardly said a prayer for the car to drive on by.

Instead it slowed down and turned into the motel's parking lot. The car was a black Chevy Impala with tinted windows, a big muscle car from the early 70's. Its engine roared throatily as it headed straight toward the lobby.

"Goddammit!"

Chip let go of the doorknob and retreated to a position behind the desk. He gave the desk's surface another quick once-over with the towel and then hurriedly did his best to mop up the small puddle on the floor. The bloody towel went into the lost-and-found box. So did the phone after he ripped the cord from the wall jack. He popped back up from behind the desk in the same instant the lobby door opened.

And then his mouth dropped open in utter astonishment.

27

The woman who walked through the door was one of the hottest he'd seen in his life. She was tall, blonde, and had a statuesque build. Her attire was skimpy—a tiny, form-fitting white tank top and denim cutoffs so brief they were barely larger than the bottom piece of a bikini—and she was profusely tattooed. On top of all that, she had the face of a goddess, with high cheekbones and deliciously plump lips rendered glossy by a shade of pink lipstick. She looked like a Hollywood version of a badass rock and roll chick or stripper, way hotter and less used-looking than the real thing often was. This was just a top-shelf example of womanly perfection all the way around. Chip wouldn't have believed anything could distract him from his dire predicament, but this woman had done it, at least temporarily.

He cleared his throat. "Um...hello. How may I, uh...help you?"

The woman removed her sunglasses as she approached the desk. "I need a room."

"Uh, well, you've come to the right place." He made himself smile, an expression that felt ghoulish given what he'd just done to Hernandez, but smiling was what a motel worker was supposed to do when a potential guest arrived. "This being a motel and all."

The woman leaned over the desk far enough to give Chip a full once-over. Chip got an eyeful of cleavage so spectacular it made him feel faint. The woman shook her head, clucking her disapproval of his attire.

She stood up straight and said, "What's your name, boy?"

"Chip."

Oh, fuck.

Chip realized he might have to use the golf club. He hadn't meant to give the woman his real name. He'd been too entranced by her looks to remember to stick to fiction. Beating a living work of art like this woman with a club struck him as an offense against nature, but if she kept being so nosy, he might not have a choice.

"How much for a room, Chip?"

"Um…"

That was a really good question. Chip's mind blanked for a moment as he resumed his impression of a drooling idiot. Then he had a memory flash of talking to Hernandez's nephew when he checked in. He forced another smile. "Fifty dollars."

"Huh."

Chip laughed. "I know. Seems like a lot for such a dump, right?"

The woman smirked. "You always badmouth your place of employment, Chip? It's bad form, if you ask me. Without that paycheck, you wouldn't be able to afford those fabulous pink flip-flops."

"Um…"

"Are you gay, Chip?"

He gave his head a shake so adamant it nearly broke his neck. "No, ma'am."

The woman laughed. "Maybe I believe you and maybe I don't. But there's one way you can prove it to me."

Chip frowned. "How's that?"

She smiled. "Pay for my room out of your own pocket."

Despite the smile, she didn't appear to be joking. Chip opened his mouth to tell her management wouldn't allow it, but then he remembered he wasn't a real employee of the Mongoose Lodge. "You know what? I'll do it."

She reached across the desk and patted his cheek, the physical contact sending a shiver of desire sizzling through him. "I know you will, Chip. I can tell you're my kind of guy. You know what? You should probably pay me."

"What?"

She shrugged and arched an eyebrow. "I made your day the second I walked in here. Don't insult me by denying it. You'll be spanking it to this memory for the rest of your life. I'd say that's worth something, wouldn't you agree?

Chip could only laugh in pure amazement. This woman was easily the most full of herself chick he'd ever met. She made Liza seem demure by comparison and that was really saying something. With the exception of his comatose girlfriend, he'd always kind of hated people so blatantly in love with themselves. But he couldn't hate her for the simple fact that she wasn't wrong. This was one of those ultra-rare cases where self-idolization was warranted. She was a goddess. He would give her money if he had it.

Oh, wait.

He looked at the cash register. It was the old-fashioned, non-computerized kind. He wasn't sure how to open it, which would be kind of hard to explain. He could tell her it was broken, but that wouldn't help because cash payments from guests would obviously have to go somewhere, right? He started to sweat a little as the moments continued to slip by with no plausible explanation presenting itself.

Then he thought of something. "Hold on. I'll be right back."

She smiled. "Don't be long. I'll get lonely."

"Be just a second."

Chip opened the door to the office, taking care to block her view of its interior with his body. Then he slipped inside and closed the door behind him. Hernandez had regained consciousness during his absence. He was sitting up and trying to scoot toward the desk, perhaps in hopes he could find some tool inside it to saw through the duct tape. His eyes got big behind the thick glasses when he saw Chip and he tried to talk through the duct tape. The tape made it impossible to understand what he was saying, but his agitation was clear.

Goddammit.

Chip didn't have time for this. He lifted a heavy hardback dictionary off the desk and whacked Hernandez in the head with it twice. Hernandez pitched over with a muffled squeal of pain. Chip set the book down and stomped on his head.

Hernandez was very still now. He might actually have killed the poor bastard this time. The guilt he felt at the prospect was only a dim echo of what he'd experienced before, which was partly because of the increasingly precarious nature of the situation. It was also because his capacity for empathy seemed to have diminished. Chip didn't like that idea, but he thought it was true. Or maybe the exposure to that insanely gorgeous woman had temporarily muted that part of him.

Speaking of...

He went to the door and opened it a crack again, relief flooding through him when he saw her still standing there on the opposite side of the desk. She seemed utterly unfazed by the sounds of scuffling. "Sorry about the noise. I'm just looking for something."

She stared right at him but did not say a word. It was hard to read her expression because she'd put the dark sunglasses on again, but she didn't seem at all nervous. Her lack of verbal response unsettled him, though, and he closed the door again.

Chip knelt next to Hernandez and rolled him onto his side. The man's girth meant he had to strain a little, but the bulge he spied in one of his rear pockets made the effort worth it. He reached into the pocket and extracted a black leather wallet. He let go of Hernandez and the old man flopped over onto his back. He still wasn't moving at all. Chip considered checking his pulse again, but he decided he'd rather not confirm what his gut was already telling him.

The wallet contained the man's driver's license and the usual array of credit cards. Chip left these alone, knowing they would be useless to him. He didn't know the man's PIN numbers and anyway cops would have too easy a time tracing use of them. In the billfold, however, he found more than two-hundred dollars in cash.

Bingo.

He pocketed half of it and folded the rest into his palm.

The woman smiled in a knowing way when he at last returned from the office and presented her with a hundred dollars in mixed bills. She sorted through them and looked at Chip. "Give me the rest of it."

He frowned. "What?"

Her eyes conveyed a coldness that hadn't been there before. She had a hand inside the shiny black handbag hanging from her shoulder. There were a hundred possible benign reasons for that, but Chip knew they were all bullshit. She had a gun in there. He didn't need to see it to know it was there. He sensed it so powerfully it was almost as if he'd suddenly been gifted with X-ray vision.

"You took that money from the guy you've got tied up back there. Don't bore me by denying it. You didn't quite get all the blood up from the floor, by the way." She shook her head in mock admonishment. "Sloppy. You kept some of that money for yourself. I know you did because that's what I would do. But life's not fair, Chip. You don't get to keep any of it."

He sighed. "But I need it. I don't have anything else."

She nodded. "I know you don't, Chip, but I'm sure you'll figure something out. Put the money on the counter and back away."

Chip saw there was no point arguing with her. Had he really thought she was an idealized Hollywood version of a female badass? The impression seemed hopelessly naïve now. She was the real deal. Chip put the money on the counter. "There really a gun in your bag or is this just an epic fake-out job?"

The woman scooped up the money and counted it before folding the wad of rumpled bills and dropping them in the bag. "You'll never know for sure." She smiled at his stricken expression. "Count yourself lucky. This could have gone much worse for you."

Chip didn't doubt it. "So you won't actually be staying here, I guess."

She smiled and strutted away from him, turning abruptly at the lobby door to address him one last time. "That was the original plan, but you've got to be adaptable in this game, Chip. I reckon whatever it is you've done here will bring a lot of heat down on this place real soon. So my friends and I will head down the road a bit and find somewhere else to stay. I recommend you be on your way soon, too."

And then she was gone, the bell above the door signaling her departure.

Chip let out a big, shuddery breath.

Goddamn.

He had just been mugged by a tattooed superbabe while in the process of committing a far more serious crime of his own. That had to be some kind of landmark in the annals of crime. Against his better judgment—which seemed to have permanently deserted him, anyway—he lifted the partition plank at the side of the desk and raced to the door, hoping for one last look at the bombshell mugger.

His heart sank when he saw she was already in the car. The tinted windows made it impossible to see inside it. There was a vanity plate attached to the big Impala's front bumper. It was the novelty type you could get at certain chintzy gift shops, the kind popular in beachside tourist towns. This one showed a pink heart against a black background. Written in a curvy script was a single word: "Dez."

The car backed away from the lobby entrance. It turned around in the empty Mongoose Lodge parking lot and drove away. Feeling a weird sense of loss, Chip returned to the desk and took a look at the floor behind it. The woman (Dez?) had been right. He had missed a few drops of blood. They were small enough you almost couldn't recognize them as blood, not without taking a close look, which she had probably done while he was busy roughing up Hernandez in the office. It was possible she'd even gotten a look at the bloody towel and phone stashed beneath the desk.

Chip stood there and thought things over a moment longer. He thought about Hernandez and he thought about Violet's body in room 1024. He thought about all the evidence he'd hoped to clean up before leaving this place. But he now recognized the notion as hopeless and a waste of time. If the incident with Dez—or whatever her name was—had taught him nothing else, it was that. Anyway, he had never been arrested and had never been in the military. His prints weren't in the system. Not yet. If he ever got picked up for anything else, he would be fucked when they took his prints and ran them through the system, because they would surely match prints lifted from this place by the crime scene investigators who would be swarming over it soon. Until then, there was a good chance he could be in the clear for the foreseeable future. He'd just have to make damn sure he never got arrested.

He grabbed the golf club and walked out of the motel into the warm afternoon sunshine.

28

The Hyundai was an older model, boxier and less attractive than the newer ones. The red paint covering it was cheap and huge patches of it had flaked away in several places. Though the ashtray beneath the nonfunctional cassette player was empty, the car's interior reeked of cigarettes. The odor was so thick and pervasive it was difficult to bear, even for an occasional smoker like Chip. Someone—either Hernandez or a previous owner—had spent many years chain-smoking his way through multiple packs a day in this thing. In addition, the car had a stick shift. He could drive stick, but he'd only done it rarely and didn't like it much. The sooner he could ditch this heap and score a new ride, the better. Hanging on to Hernandez's car very long wouldn't be a good idea anyway, but for now it was a necessary evil.

After some aggravating adventures in slipping the clutch, he got the Hyundai out on the road and pointed it in the direction of the convenience store where Violet's probable murderer worked. It was unlikely she was there now, but the store was the only lead he had on her. His plan was to talk to whoever was on duty and find out where she lived. If the person was reluctant to cough up the information, he would have to beat it out of them.

Violence would be the last resort, but he would do whatever necessary to get what he wanted. The thought caused him barely any anxiety. It was funny how quickly a person could get used to a thing formerly so distasteful. Actually, there was nothing funny about it. It fucking sucked. At this point, his actions made him no better than Liza.

There were two other cars in the parking lot—a silver minivan parked at the pump and a blue Chevy Malibu parked at the edge of the lot. Given its placement, he assumed the Malibu was driven by the Kwik-Stop employee on duty today. The car's color made his heart race a little faster at first as he recalled the sedan driven by the only other guest at the Mongoose Lodge last night. But that had been a four-door sedan. This was a smaller two-door car and the shade of blue was a little darker.

Chip parked on the opposite side of the pump from the minivan, the side facing the store, which made it harder to see from the road, a potential lifesaver if Hernandez's body was discovered during his interrogation of the store clerk. He got out of the Hyundai and started toward the store, feeling conspicuously ridiculous in his shabby attire. The flap of the flip-flops against the asphalt felt particularly shameful. But this was an attitude he had to ditch if he hoped to come across as sufficiently intimidating. In the wake of what he'd done to Hernandez, he felt up to the task. Until today he'd never been anything like a brutalizing hardass, but life was teaching him some quick lessons in how to be a bastard.

He took a quick look around as he entered the store, confirming what he'd already suspected—he and the clerk were the only people inside the Kwik-Stop. The soccer mom driving the minivan was sitting inside the vehicle in air-conditioned comfort while the gas nozzle was set to fill its tank automatically. There was no point in fucking around. He had to get right to it, get the information he needed fast, and go find that thieving bitch.

The skinny girl from last night had been passably cute, despite her virtually nonexistent figure. The clerk behind the counter today was another story. She was a large girl in her late teens or early twenties and she had a slow-witted, dull-eyed look about her. She was missing enough teeth to peg her as either a current or former meth user. The name on the tag pinned to her shirt was Amy Hayworth.

Chip walked up to the counter and said, "Hey. Amy, right?"

"That's right."

Chip smiled. "Amy, I was hoping you could help me with something. I'm looking for the girl who was working the overnight shift here last night. Skinny. Dark hair. You know who I mean."

Amy nodded. "Yeah. Monica Delacroix."

Chip did a double-take at the revelation of the skinny girl's surname. He didn't recall noting it during his previous visit to the Kwik-Stop, but he supposed it had entered his subconscious anyway, which explained why it had popped into his head during his check-in at the Mongoose Lodge a short while later. Though this was an interesting insight, it wasn't exactly crucial knowledge. Much more interesting was how fast Amy had given up her co-worker's name. It meant getting the information he needed might not be as difficult as he had feared.

"Do you know where I can find Monica?"

Amy's brow creased. "Aren't you a little old to be sniffing after that bitch?"

Chip strove to keep his smile good-natured. "Hell, I'm not even quite thirty yet. Don't make me out to be ancient, Amy. You could hurt a guy's feelings that way."

This earned a big smile from Amy. "You ain't so bad-looking for an old guy."

"Well, thanks. You're quite a looker, too."

"Wanna go in the back and get a blowjob?"

The offer so took Chip by surprise that he could only gape at her for a moment before replying. "Uh...while that's a tempting offer, it's really important I talk to Monica soon."

"What about?"

"It's private business, I'm sorry. But if you can tell me where she is, you'd really be doing me a huge favor."

Amy Hayworth smirked. The shift in her expression made her seem less slow-witted than Chip initially suspected, which made him uneasy. "I can tell you exactly where to find that whore. I hate her, by the way. I don't even care if you're a stalker or something. Cut her goddamn head off, I don't give a shit. But the info will cost you."

Chip sighed.

Of course.

There was something about this store, something in the very air that made its female employees want to take advantage of him. Perhaps the manager had a practice of only hiring girls with a prior history of blackmail convictions.

"What do you want, Amy?"

"Oh, I think you know."

She came out from behind the counter and extended a hand. Chip eyed the pudgy fingers with distaste. He didn't have a problem with larger girls in general—often they were quite sexy—but this one's overall slovenliness, coupled with her meth mouth, made the notion of any kind of intimacy with her a deeply unattractive proposition.

"If we do this, you'll tell me where to find Monica?"

Amy shook her head. "Jesus, you're slow. Ain't that what I already said?"

Chip grimaced. Yes. Of course it was.

He took her hand. "Lead the way."

Amy led him through a flapping black door into the store's back room. She dragged Chip over to a stack of beer crates, positioned him against them, and dropped to her knees in front of him.

She cupped his crotch and grinned up at him. "Ready for the blowjob of your life?"

Chip didn't say anything, had no concept of what he might say even if he wanted to say something. This girl repulsed him and he strongly doubted he could get it up for her. He hoped the fact he was letting her try would in itself be enough to satisfy her. If she got mad, he could tell her he was gay and was never able to perform with girls, even ones as sexy as she was.

Amy tugged down the sweatpants and drew his flaccid cock into her mouth. To his surprise, he began to get hard almost immediately. Not rock hard, the way he was with women he was genuinely attracted to, but there was definitely something happening, which surprised the shit out of him. That he was responding at all baffled him and he was at first at a loss to explain it. Some of it was her unexpected oral skills. It turned out she'd had some good cause to brag. She manipulated him as expertly as anyone ever had, with the kind of talent that only came from lots and lots of practice. Even her nasty teeth were never an issue as he hardly ever felt them. Chip closed his eyes and turned his head up toward the ceiling. In blackness, it was possible to pretend some angelic beauty was blowing him.

Someone like...

Chip's eyes snapped open.

Someone like Dez.

Which might not even be her name, but he knew he would forever think of her as Dez, thanks to that vanity plate. She was the real reason for the unexpected arousal. He remembered how she'd mocked him, saying he would be spanking it to her memory for the rest of his life. He hadn't doubted the truth of the prediction for even a second. And the moment he thought of her, his cock turned almost painfully hard in Amy's mouth, earning an appreciative groan from her.

Chip closed his eyes again and allowed his mind to fill with a crystal-clear image of Dez standing there in the lobby of the Mongoose Lodge. Every lovely, devastating detail came vividly back to him. The long, toned legs. The flare of her hips. The narrowness of her waist. The jut of her beautiful breasts. Her plump, pink lips. All those colorful tattoos…

He pictured Dez going down on him behind the reception desk at the motel.

Pictured those glistening pink lips wrapped around—

Chip screamed at the shock of sudden orgasm and Amy made excited, slurping noises as her mouth filled with his ejaculate.

29

The trailer park where Monica Delacroix lived with her meth-dealing boyfriend was a fifteen-minute ride from the Kwik-Stop. Chip had to get out on the interstate and take the westbound ramp going toward Nashville. He pulled off the interstate again two exits down and, once he reached the main road off the highway, took a left turn down a winding stretch of two-lane rural blacktop. The landscape around this interstate junction was even more desolate than the one that had led him first to Monica and then to the Mongoose Lodge. Thinking about that, he was struck by how capricious life could be, how so much could turn on the simple choices people made every day. If he had taken any other exit last night, Violet would still be alive and he wouldn't be on this insane hunt to reclaim the money. It didn't seem fair in the least, but he knew even thinking about such things in terms of "fairness" was childish. To win at anything in this life, you needed luck and a willingness to fuck the other person before they could fuck you.

According to Amy Hayworth, the trailer park was some five miles down this road after turning off the interstate. The road was shrouded by tall trees on both sides. In that respect, it was similar to the back road that had carried him out to Echo's deserted rental house. The daylight was a mixed blessing. It meant he didn't have to drive almost blind on an unfamiliar ribbon of backwoods road. But a daytime approach to Monica's residence was risky. He'd much prefer to go in at night, when the darkness would allow for greater stealth. Unfortunately, he didn't have the luxury of waiting that long. He was riding around in a probable murder victim's car and the need to ditch the Hyundai as soon as possible remained urgent.

He kept an eye on the odometer as the miles rolled away. Once he neared five miles traveled since turning off the interstate, he focused his attention on the left-hand side of the road, where Amy had told him he would see the entrance to Monica's trailer park. He became anxious when the five-mile mark passed with no sign of the place, but he reminded himself that the distance was only Amy's rough estimate. There was no reason to panic yet. When he came around a sharp bend in the road, there was a break in the trees to the left and the trailer park revealed itself.

It wasn't much, just two rows of four trailers with a wide dirt lane between the rows. He turned off the dirt lane and eased into the space between the second and third trailers on the right. Monica's trailer was the last one on this side. An old Buick was parked outside the trailer to his right. There was also a propane-fueled grill and a picnic table with empty bottles of Miller High Life scattered across its top. Someone was home there. Chip hoped it was some redneck still sleeping off a night of drinking beers under the stars.

The trailer to his left appeared unoccupied. There were no cars parked outside and the windows were dark. Chip pulled around its side and parked there. He grabbed the golf club, got out of the Hyundai, and took a quick look around. There was no one in the vicinity and as far as he could tell he'd arrived unobserved.

He approached the trailer's corner and took a careful peek around it for his first look at the humble Delacroix abode. Three cars were parked outside it—a Mustang, a Dodge Neon with lots of paint flaking off it, and a familiar-looking tan-colored Pontiac. He felt a rush of adrenaline upon spying the Pontiac. He'd doubted the trustworthiness of Amy's information, but it looked like she'd been honest with him. As grossed-out as he'd been by the experience on one level, it seemed allowing her to blow him had been a wise investment.

Chip edged around the corner a little more, checking the area to see if anyone was around before making his final approach. There was no one in sight. It was possible someone watching from the window of another trailer might spot him, but that was a chance he had to take. The situation was about as optimal as he could reasonably hope.

Chip let out a breath.

All right, he thought. *Let's do this.*

He stepped out of his sheltered spot and approached Monica's trailer as rapidly as possible, cursing the damn flip-flops all the way. You couldn't really run in them—not well, anyway—and they weren't the kind of footwear you needed when you hoped to come across like some crazy, hardcase motherfucker. A nice pair of boots would be best for a job like this. Boots like the pair Monica and her male friend had stolen from him.

Chip got angry again when he thought about all that had been taken from him. The boots were the least of it, but he meant to have them again, too, goddammit. His boots, his clothes, his wallet, the fucking money, and Liza's Pontiac, which was really his Pontiac now, seeing how she was in a coma and all. He was taking it all back and God help anyone who tried to stop him.

As he neared the steps leading to the trailer's front door, he took another quick look around and was relieved to find himself still alone. He mounted the steps and raised a hand to test the doorknob. He hoped he wouldn't have to kick it open, but he figured it wouldn't be much of a problem if that's what he had to do. The door looked flimsy, which was in keeping with the rest of the trailer's shambolic external appearance. There were piles of junk stacked up in front of the trailer and trash was strewn everywhere. The yard around Monica's trailer was by far the worst-kept in the entire park. He wondered whether the other residents ever bitched to the manager about the state of the place. Maybe they had and maybe they hadn't, and maybe the manager just didn't care. It wasn't like any of them were living at the Ritz.

The door came open before his hand could close around the knob.

A skinny blond kid in a white wife-beater shirt grinned and pointed a gun at him.

30

The kid eyed the golf club clutched in Chip's hand and laughed, revealing a case of meth mouth even grimmer than the one afflicting Amy Hayworth. Virtually all of his front teeth were gone, except for a lone holdout on the bottom. How the guy could eat anything other than soft foods was a mystery to Chip. Equally perplexing was why Monica Delacroix would shack up with such a loser. She was no Miss America candidate, but she had an appealing face and she did have all her teeth.

However, the answers to these mysteries didn't matter much to Chip, who was again ruing both his stupidity and rotten luck. He should have recognized the impossibility of getting the money back. These people were armed, out of their minds on drugs, and had likely been waiting for him to come after them all day. There was a spare key in a magnetic container clamped to the Pontiac's underside. He should have just taken the car and hauled ass out of here. There might have been just enough gas left in the car's tank to get him back home. Doing that and writing the money off would have been the smart way to go.

But he'd stopped doing smart things a while ago. So…here he was.

The kid tilted his chin at him. "Were you planning to tee off on me with that thing, asshole?" He laughed heartily, giving Chip another good look at the blackened nubs at the back of his mouth. "You get it, fuckface? 'Tee off'?"

More idiot laughter.

Chips hands tightened on the club's grip. His one chance here was immediate, brutal action, just like with Hernandez back at the Mongoose Lodge. He needed to strike fast while this shithead was so focused on how funny he thought this was. But the ability to act with deadly and unhesitating efficiency seemed to have deserted him. Mostly it was because of the gun pointing right at his face. He could see that its safety was off. Also, there was one more step up into the trailer, which gave the kid an additional tactical advantage. Chip would have to swing up at him and hope to connect in just the right way before the gun could discharge.

The kid's amused grin faded and he eyed Chip more warily. "Oh, hell, you're still thinking of taking a swing at me, aren't you? Stupid cocksucker."

Chip didn't answer. There was no need.

The kid extended his arm and held it a little more rigidly. The gun's sight was now lined up with the space between Chip's eyes. "Drop the club, douchebag."

Immediate compliance seemed in order, but Chip stood there frozen a moment longer. Being forced to surrender his only weapon was hard to accept. He still couldn't believe this mental midget had the upper hand over him. It was just more evidence of the universe deliberately fucking with him. Someone up there was repeatedly allowing him the tiniest glimmer of hope...only to then throw up some new and thoroughly unexpected roadblock just when it finally looked like he had things under some semblance of control. Anything that could possibly go wrong *was* going wrong.

The kid sneered at his hesitation. "I *will* blow your brains out, motherfucker. You got to the count of three to drop that thing. One, two—"

Chip let go of the club and it struck the fiberglass steps with a clatter before bouncing to the ground.

The kid moved back a couple steps and said, "Welcome to our happy home, asshole."

Chip considered turning tail and making a dash for the Hyundai. It wasn't that far away. The kid would undoubtedly start popping off rounds at him right away. The prospect of getting shot in the back held no appeal at all. But maybe the guy was a bad shot. He'd heard somewhere that handguns were only good against a moving target at close range. If he could put a little bit of distance himself and the trailer before the guy could squeeze off his first shot, he might have some small sliver of a chance. He'd need some luck on his side—and luck had been in short supply of late—but that small chance had to be preferable to whatever these people had in mind for him inside the trailer.

The kid smirked. "I know what you're thinking. And I'd shoot you down before you got two steps away. Don't be a dumbass."

Chip figured he was about to be a dumbass, anyway. There was no real choice here. But just as he was about to bolt, his ears picked up the sound of an approaching engine. The kid's eyes flicked to a spot behind Chip, who turned his head and squinted against the glare of the sun to see a blue Chevy Malibu roaring up to the trailer.

The car pulled up almost right against the steps, putting yet another roadblock—this one more literal than most—between Chip and any chance at a relatively happy outcome. The driver's side door opened and Amy Hayworth got out clutching a forty-ounce bottle of Colt .45 malt liquor. "Yo, Leroy, you're not starting the party without me, are you?"

The blond kid laughed. "You're just in time."

Amy ascended the first step and put a hand against the small of Chip's back. "Go on in, honey. You know you're not going anywhere."

Chip sighed in defeat and stepped up into the trailer. He knew he shouldn't feel shocked by Amy's duplicity, but he sort of was anyway. She'd seemed so sincere in her avowed hatred of Monica, but it'd all been an act, a very skilled one at that. He was feeling more and more like a hopeless rube with each passing moment. Clearly he wasn't cut out for this crime thing. If getting outsmarted by a bunch of meth-abusing teenagers wasn't proof enough of that, he couldn't imagine what would be.

Once they were all inside the trailer, Amy shut and locked the door.

Chip looked at her and said, "You called ahead and told them to expect me, didn't you?"

She screwed the cap off the bottle of Colt .45 and took a big swig. "Wow, you're a fucking genius. You figured it out. Congratulations."

Then she kicked him in the balls. Chip howled in pain and staggered backward a few steps before tripping up and falling to the floor. He wouldn't have believed the rotund bitch capable of executing a move like that with such precision and force. The threadbare sweatpants had offered little in the way of protection, but he suspected he'd be in agony even if he'd been wearing a cup.

Everyone in the trailer's dingy living room was laughing at him. This included Amy and Leroy and two other people he'd never seen before, a guy and a gal who were sitting on a ratty green sofa. The two on the sofa were a slightly plump blonde girl with big tits and a scrawny guy with close-cropped brown hair and lots of tats on his arms and neck. Like Leroy, this guy wore a white wife-beater. He had his arm around the blonde's shoulders. They were both watching him with disturbingly avid expressions. Chip guessed they were excited about the prospect of watching—or perhaps participating in—whatever was about to happen to him. That was the moment he began to suspect his fate involved something more than a quick and simple execution. They were going to torture him.

Amy moved past him and dropped onto an unoccupied section of the sofa. Her weight caused the edge of the cushion beneath her to rise sharply upward. She shot a smirk in Leroy's direction. "Closed the store to be here for this shit. Better be worth it."

Leroy snorted. "Won't you get in trouble?"

"Nah. Called Darnell to cover for me. He'll be there soon." Amy raised her voice to ear-splitting volume. *"Where my bitch at!?"*

A high-pitched reply came from behind a closed door: *"Give me a goddamn minute!"*

The trailer was comprised of just three main rooms—the living room, which took up the bulk of the space, a kitchen at one end with an adjacent little dining area, and a bedroom at the opposite end of the trailer. Monica emerged from the bedroom a few moments after her shrill reply to Amy's grammatically questionable query. She was wearing tight cotton shorts and nothing else. A fat guy who looked like he was probably in his late forties followed her into the living room. His big gut strained against a Dale Earnhardt T-shirt. The guy spared Chip only a fleeting glance as he walked past him and out of the trailer. No help would be coming from that direction. It'd be nice to imagine the guy might do the right thing and call the cops—who now represented a marginally less terrifying fate—but no way was that gonna happen.

Leroy snickered. "Cody give it to you good?"

"Could barely get it up. As usual."

The scrawny guy on the sofa said, "You still fucking for cash even though you're rich now?"

Monica shrugged. "Easy money. And I'm *not* rich. This was a good score, but it's not retirement money." She sensed Chip staring at her and turned in his direction, thrusting her pert little breasts at him. "Enjoying the scenery? You should. They're the last tits you'll ever see."

Amy cackled. "Maybe I'll let him see mine. He'd like them, I bet. Already gave him a hummer. He shot so much jizz into my mouth I almost choked on it." The scrawny guy on the sofa made a disgusted sound. "Gross."

Monica pulled on a Hooters T-shirt, which struck Chip as funny given her relative deficiency in the area of mammary endowment. Maybe it was purposeful irony. She was the sharpest of this bunch, he was pretty sure. It was possible she had a subtler wit than one would think. "You want to give this idiot a show, go ahead. I don't think he's worth it, personally."

Amy rolled her eyes. "Come on. You got to admit he's easy on the eyes."

Monica shrugged. "Maybe, but he's dumb. I don't like dumb guys. Besides, he won't look too good once we're done with him."

The comment elicited more laughter. This time it was imbued with an even more disturbing edge. The sadomasochistic glee evident in the demeanors of each of these walking white trash clichés was shocking. Despite the brutality of the acts she'd committed, even Liza hadn't seemed turned on by the idea of murder. But then he wondered about that, recalling how they'd stopped for that roadside fuck shortly after fleeing the McKenzies' house. And he remembered his own excitement following his initial trepidation. It'd been their most frenzied coupling in some time. Thinking about that in conjunction with his current situation made him wonder if all humans were monsters not so far beneath the surface. And being called dumb by Monica got under his skin.

He could take insults like that from Liza, but hearing the same crap from this thieving bitch was another story. He wanted to put his hands around that slender neck of hers and squeeze until her eyes bulged out and her face turned blue.

Monica tilted her head, squinting at him in a curious way as she appeared to read his thoughts. "Oh, wow. I do believe the poor little dummy is pissed at me."

The others laughed again, but there was a strangely nervous quality to their laughter this time. Chip thought it had something to do with how Monica's tone was now missing its previous tinge of demented mirth. He hadn't sensed it before, but he saw it clearly now—this was a person possessed of a volcanic, terrifying temper. It was why the others now seemed to fear her despite their own dearth of basic humanity.

Monica's features twisted with fury as she came at him fast and kicked him in the face. The heel of her foot slammed into his nose, breaking it with an audible snap that made most of the leering onlookers gasp. Chip screamed in pain and rolled away from her. It felt like someone had jammed a spear through the center of his head, the agony was so massive. And it didn't help that she kept coming at him, allowing him no peace and no time to recuperate as she relentlessly pressed the attack. One kick to his groin nearly succeeded in crushing his balls again and when he swatted at her leg in instinctive self-defense, she unleashed a scream of outrage so searing it made his ears ring. She was furious with him for having the gall to defend himself, even in so pitiful a manner. And she made him pay for it dearly by successfully landing another kick to his nose. It didn't connect with as much force this time, but it didn't need to—the damage had already been done. And now the pain was such that it made him sob and brought tears streaming from his eyes.

She finally broke off the attack when his tears started, but she didn't do it out of compassion. Chip blinked his tears away and saw her smile of perverse satisfaction. "Give me the gun, Leroy."

Leroy flipped it to her and she caught in midair. It struck Chip as a really reckless way to handle a firearm, but then these weren't exactly safety-first type people. Monica knelt next to him and put the gun against his forehead. "Ready to die?"

Chip could only sob in response. The pain hadn't subsided enough to allow anything else.

Monica laughed. "You're a fucking pussy, you know that?"

Chip shuddered and let out a breath. "Just kill me. Be done with it."

Monica flipped hair out of her eyes. She laughed again as her features arranged themselves in an expression of mock sympathy. "Aw, you're already giving up? Is there no fight in you at all? Man, you really *are* a pussy. I almost feel sorry for you."

The others laughed, a little less nervously now.

Monica stood up.

Then Chip was in motion, acting without thought as he rolled over and launched himself at her. This happened too fast for Monica or any of her friends to prevent it. Chip slammed a shoulder into her midsection, knocking the air out of her before driving her to the floor. The gun discharged once before the force of impact sent it flying from her hand. The gunshot made the rest of them yelp in surprised terror. But Chip paid them no mind as he sat up and cocked a fist, intending to beat Monica to death with his bare hands. He was bigger and stronger than her. She was at his mercy and there was nothing she could do to stop the pummeling she was about to take. In terms of sheer strength and body mass, he outclassed all of them. It was an advantage he possessed over much of the population. He was fit and had a big, muscular frame. However, he wasn't an aggressive person by nature and rarely used his size against people. But like a lot of other things, any reservations he had in that area were now gone.

But before he could uncork a blow that would have permanently marred Monica's good looks, there was a flash of movement in his peripheral vision—and then he saw Leroy darting toward the kitchen, which was where the gun had landed. Unleashing a savage roar of rage, Chip got to his feet and went after Leroy with everything he had. He hit the kid's back like a runaway freight train, driving him all the way across the kitchen before slamming him against the edge of the counter. Other people were screaming in the living room as Leroy cried out in pain. Chip turned him around and clamped a hand around his throat, grinning savagely at the way the kid's face contorted and turned red.

Chip sensed movement behind him.

Keeping his grip on Leroy's throat, he spun them both about and saw Amy creeping toward the gun. Monica was still on the floor and the other couple looked rooted to the sofa, their mouths open in expressions of dumbfounded shock. At the moment, the only dangerous one was Amy. He had to keep her from getting the gun. The only problem was she was closer to it than he was. And her hands weren't full. So he did the only thing he could—he threw Leroy at her. The skinny meth dealer crashed into the fat girl and they both went tumbling back into the living room.

Chip scooped up the gun.

He experienced an unfamiliar feeling it took him a moment to recognize as confidence. And when he realized what the feeling was, he couldn't help grinning. At long last, the tide was turning in his favor and he'd managed to make it happen just when things had looked their bleakest. All he had to do was keep fighting and never give up. It was that determination that had brought him to the brink of recovering the money in the first place and he'd nearly forgotten it. Now all that was left was to execute all these redneck pieces of shit, recover his stuff, and get the fuck out of here.

Intending to do just that, he took a step toward the living room.

And that was when he heard a creak of unoiled hinges somewhere behind him. Chip turned his head to look in that direction. The trailer had a rear door that opened into the kitchen, a door that was swinging open now. Chip turned fully in that direction and aimed the gun at the door. His forefinger tensed around the 9mm's trigger. He belatedly recognized the gun as the one that had been stolen from him, which was fitting. The first item of his stuff he'd recovered would be the instrument via which he ended the lives of the people who'd sought to ruin his life.

The door came all the way open.

And a little blond-haired kid of about six or seven came into the kitchen with an expression of wide-eyed, trembling terror.

Chip frowned.

Shit.

Killing a bunch of scuzzy meth addicts who would've done the same to him was one thing, but this was another matter entirely. Before he could even begin to sort out what to do about it, something heavy hit the back of his head with staggering force.

31

The blow didn't quite knock him out, but it came close. He was woozy as he felt multiple sets of hands grab onto him. His eyes wanted to close, but he knew he couldn't let that happen, not if he wanted to live. He was temporarily unclear on why his life was in danger. The world around him was fuzzy and he felt disconnected from it. It was almost like being in a dream-state, yet somehow he knew he was definitely not dreaming. He tried to concentrate and realized he was moving, sliding. He needed another moment to realize he was being dragged across the floor. The people dragging him kept going in and out of focus, the shapes of their faces and bodies shifting and morphing in a kaleidoscopic way. A babble of excited voices seemed to float in the air, a drifting, echoing sound.

At some point he did close his eyes and the world went away for a bit. When he opened them again, his head was throbbing but his mind was clear. They had taken a chair with a wrought-iron frame from the kitchen and had put him in it, but they had not bound him to it. He found this curious until his vision came into focus and he saw the guns pointed at him. Leroy and the other scrawny dude in a wife-beater were the ones with the guns. His head swiveled to the left a little and he saw

Amy making out with the other scrawny guy's plump blonde girlfriend on the sofa. They looked like they were really into it. As he watched, the scrawny guy's girlfriend pushed Amy into a prone position and crawled atop her, after which the make out session resumed. Chip couldn't believe it. Amy sure seemed to get a lot of action for someone so outwardly unattractive. But he had bigger concerns that this puzzler.

Monica was nowhere in sight.

That concerned him more than the guns pointed his way. She was the clear leader of this little posse of shitheads and they wouldn't kill him without first getting the go-ahead from her. He was overcome with an intense desire to know where she was and what she was doing. He didn't hear anyone moving around in the kitchen behind him and he could detect no hint of activity in the bedroom through the wide-open door. Allowing these people to get the upper hand again after fighting back so hard and turning the tables on them was the worst possible thing that could have happened. There would be a heavy price to pay for his act of violent defiance. They'd had bad things in mind for him all along, but now it would be many times worse. Monica's terrible temper would demand it.

Seconds after he realized someone else was missing—that goddamn interloping mystery kid—the trailer's front door creaked open and Monica walked through it. She smiled when she saw Chip was awake again. He gulped when he saw what she had in her hands—the golf club he'd dropped outside. He'd meant to intimidate them into giving up the money with it, but now it would be used for another purpose.

She jabbed at Amy and the other girl with the clubhead. "Break it up, you fucking dykes. Watch me have some fun with this asshole."

Amy and the large-bosomed blonde separated and sat up on the sofa, straightening their clothes and brushing their hair back from their faces. Amy's face was flushed, but she was smiling, though whether it was from enjoyment of what she'd been doing with the cute blonde or delight at the prospect of what Monica was about to do was hard to say. She glanced in Chip's direction and the smile became the same kind of ghoulish leer he'd glimpsed earlier on all their faces.

Monica approached Chip and touched the clubhead to his knee, making him flinch. She laughed at his reaction. "Oh, don't worry. I won't start with the knees. It'd be no fun to cripple you right away."

It happened too fast to do anything about it, like maybe throwing himself to the floor to get out of the way. His thinking was still a little muddy from the blow to the head and his reflexes were non-existent. She reared back with the club and swung it in a precise, vicious arc. The clubhead smashed against his jaw, igniting a new burst of searing pain as it snapped his head violently to the side. Monica immediately swung the club a second time and it pounded against his shoulder with a crunch of bone. Chip screamed in agony and began blubbering the kind of desperate pleas that would have shamed him only a short while ago. It just hurt so fucking much. And the worst part of it was he knew she was just getting started.

He was right about that.

She swung the club again and again, targeting his ribs and his arms for the most part. She kept shifting position to aim at new areas. The clubhead pounded his hips, thighs, and shins. These all caused fresh, massive explosions of pain. His flesh was being pulverized and there were things broken inside him. His jaw was swollen. Some of his ribs felt splintered. There was a stabbing sensation in his right side that made him want to scream. Then he did scream, as loud as he could. He didn't know what was causing that stabbing feeling and didn't want to know, suspected there was nothing that could be done about it anyway. He only stopped screaming through a supreme exertion of will after Monica had the other, still-nameless scrawny guy put the barrel of his gun against the back of his head. She ordered him to be quiet or she would have her friend put a bullet through his skull. Chip knew he should just let the guy shoot him. Just be done with this, spare himself the rest of the torture he knew was coming. But he just couldn't. He was still too afraid of death.

He whimpered and hung his head as tears poured down his face. "Please...please...please..."

Monica touched the clubhead to his chin, making him flinch and squeal in fear. "Are you done screaming, asshole, or do I start swinging at your head again?"

His sobs after she voiced the question were too intense to allow him to form and push out the words. Though she could plainly see the difficulty he was having, Monica took his failure to respond as an excuse to strike him with the club again (not that she needed an excuse). The clubhead smacked against his arm. Though it wasn't anything near painless, it was one of the more restrained blows. It was, however, enough to shake loose the words she was seeking.

"I'm done screaming. I swear. Please..."

Monica touched the clubhead to his chin again, pushing his head back and forcing him to hold it up straight. She smiled. "I'm just getting started on you. We're gonna make a whole party of it. Play some music. Get drunk. Get fucking high. And I'm betting the more fucked up we get, the more fucked up the stuff we're gonna do to you will be." She laughed. "What do you think? You wanna take that bet?"

Chip sighed. "No."

Monica nodded. "I didn't think so. But I want to have a little chat with you before you're too far gone. I mean, I'm pretty fucking proud of the scam I pulled on you. That was some brilliant shit, man. If there's anything you want to know about how it went down before it's too late, now's your chance. So...you got any questions?"

Chip had plenty of questions and he was happy to indulge her in this way. Anything to delay what was coming even a little longer. And he figured he might as well start with the big one. "Did you kill Violet?"

"Yes."

"Why did you do it?"

Monica rolled her eyes. "Isn't it obvious? To take that fat roll you were flashing around at the Kwik-

Stop last night and frame you for her murder. The frame-up was so the po-po wouldn't look into any other ideas about what happened. It was all neat and tidy, see. The dead bitch is right there with her killer. End of story."

"Why don't I remember anything?"

She chuckled. "Roofies, bitch. You got a triple dose."

Jesus.

No wonder there was a big black hole where his memory should be.

Talking with a swollen jaw wasn't easy. Chip couldn't tell whether it was broken, but it definitely hurt like a bitch. His tongue felt too thick inside his dry throat. He tried to think of when he'd last had a drink of anything. It didn't seem possible that he'd gone without liquid of any type since last night, but that appeared to be the case. And now that he was aware of the deficiency, a need for something—anything—to soothe his parched throat felt urgent.

"Can I get a drink of water?"

"No."

"Aw, it's thirsty," said the blonde with the big tits.

Chip made eye contact with Monica. "Please."

She glanced at the scrawny guy standing behind him. "Get him a glass." She looked at Chip. "See? All you have to do is ask nicely like a good little boy and maybe you'll get what you want."

"Could you please let me go?"

This provoked a round of hearty laughter from Monica and her friends. They were all highly amused. The reaction was a little over-the-top, but there was a surprising honesty in it. Chip figured a stab at humor was the last thing they'd expected from a guy in his position. Amy and her make out partner even exchanged a high-five.

Even Monica was smiling in a seemingly nonmalevolent way for once. "It's too bad we didn't meet some other way, dude. You almost seem like you could be fun."

Chip tried to smile, but it hurt like hell and probably looked more like a grimace. "I'm a *lot* of fun. Look, there's no reason we can't be friends. You can keep the money. You fucking earned it as far as I'm concerned. Just let me take my car and give me back my clothes, and we'll call it even, all right?"

Monica shook her head. "Can't do that. I'd kind of like to, because this has all been a blast, but there's no way I'd trust you not to come back another time and make another grab for the money. And I know you're not gonna forget what I did to your girl. Who would? I'd want revenge, too, in your place. No, man, we gotta kill you."

The scrawny guy returned from the kitchen with a tall plastic glass filled to the brim. Just seeing the water made Chip's thirst significantly worse. He *ached* for it. The scrawny guy tried to give the glass to Monica, but she sneered at him and tilted her head at Chip. "Did *I* ask for water, dumbass? Just give it to him. Jesus, Matt."

A hurt look flashed across Matt's face, but he did as she said, handing the glass to Chip, who put it to his mouth and grimaced as he tilted his head back. He drained its contents in several large, rapid swallows. Once the last drop had been consumed, he heaved a big breath and said, "I don't guess I could trouble you for one more glass?"

Monica responded with a single firm shake of her head.

Matt plucked the glass from his fingers and took it back into the kitchen.

Leroy was getting antsy. He stretched his neck out and scratched at it with the sight of the gun. He had a finger inside the trigger guard, curled around the trigger. Chip noted that the safety was still off. He hoped the idiot would exert a little too much pressure and blow his stupid brains out. No such luck. "We done playing nice with this fool?" He nodded at the golf club. "Let me take a turn at him with that thing."

Monica glared at him. "This is my game. We're playing it by my rules. Besides, you'd just beat him to death inside of five minutes. I want to make this shit last."

Hearing the torture he was enduring referred to as a "game" caused the already profound sense of despair gripping Chip to intensify enough to open the floodgates again. His bottom lip trembled uncontrollably and fresh tears poured down his cheeks. He cringed when Monica tapped the clubhead against the side of his head.

"Any last questions before we have some more fun with you?"

Chip scrambled to think of something. These people were eager for Monica to resume the game. He remained equally as eager to delay it as long as possible. His breath came in quick gasps as an extreme state of panic briefly paralyzed his brain. His eyes got wide as Monica drew the club back and flexed her fingers around its grip. His gaze flicked from the heavy clubhead to her flinty eyes and back again several times. A smile of almost sexual anticipation curved the corners of her mouth.

"I'll take your silence as a 'no', Chip."

"Wait!"

Monica smirked. "No more fucking around. If you've got a question, ask it. *Now.*"

Chip gaped at her, his brain still maddeningly frozen—and then he thought of something. "How did you find us? After we left the Kwik-Stop, I mean."

"Oh, that was easy. I saw you drive off in the direction of the Mongoose, so that's where I looked for you. If you'd gone on down the road, your bitch would still be alive and none of this would be happening." She smiled. "Funny how life works sometimes, huh?"

"What about my clothes? And my wallet? Why take them?"

"Didn't want you fleeing the scene. Figured that'd be the easiest way to keep you there."

Chip frowned. "But that doesn't make sense. The cops would wonder what happened to all my stuff. Hell, it'd probably cast doubt on my guilt, maybe make them more likely to buy the idea of a frame-up."

Monica shrugged. "I admit that part wasn't as well thought-out as the rest of it. Nobody's perfect, man.

We were high as shit and it seemed like a good idea at the time. Anything else?"

"That kid earlier...who was he?"

She smiled. "Just this cute little brat who likes to come by and play Xbox sometimes. His mom is a refugee from that stupid Wandering Souls cult in Nashville. Which is funny, because she pretty much lets him wander wherever he wants. I walked him home and told him I'd buy him an Xbox of his very own if he keeps quiet about what he saw."

Leroy snickered. "Shit, let's let him have our old system and buy ourselves a new one with Happy Gilmore's money."

He was referring, of course, to the Adam Sandler movie *Happy Gilmore*, which, among other things, was about a guy who enjoyed golf.

How fucking clever, asshole.

Monica brought the clubhead slowly around and placed it against Chip's ear. "Interview's over, bitch. You ready to hurt some more?"

"Please—"

Monica's expression turned hard. "Shut up."

With no further hesitation, she drew the club back again and swung it around with all her might. As Chip watched the arc of the clubhead, he wanted nothing more than to get out of the way, but Leroy and Matt had the guns trained on him again so that wasn't possible. The clubhead smashed against his ear, making him shriek in agony. It was the hardest she'd struck him yet. He realized now she'd been holding back earlier. It was like she'd said—she wanted to draw this thing out as long as she could. Now, however, she was apparently ready to ramp up the intensity.

The club whickered through the air again and struck him in the neck. This time he couldn't scream because of the placement of the blow and fell gagging out of the chair. Two sets of hands immediately hauled him up off the floor and slammed him back into the chair. Monica resumed the attack as soon as he was seated again. This time she finally targeted a knee, the muscles in her neck standing out as the clubhead bounced hard off his kneecap. The pain was excruciating and Chip couldn't help screaming.

Monica hit him with the club at least a dozen more times. Then, apparently tiring of it, she tossed the club aside. "Somebody put on some music. And somebody else go buy a bunch of booze. I don't care who does what so long as somebody keeps an eye on that piece of shit in the chair. But don't do anything else to him until I say so." She looked at Amy and crooked a finger at her. "You…come with me."

With a grunt of effort, Amy pushed herself off the sofa and waddled over to Monica. They joined hands and retreated to the bedroom, shutting the door behind them. Leroy and Matt exchanged smirks as they glanced at each other. The blonde girl stared at the closed door with an expression of longing or hurt, Chip couldn't say which. The precise nature of the relationships in play here was hard to guess at, but his pain was too total and too unrelenting to care much.

The blonde sighed and shifted her attention to her male friends. "So who's gonna get the beer?"

Leroy dug into a pocket and threw some bills at her. "You, that's who. Now get out of here."

She slid off the sofa and scooped up the money. "What kind of beer do you want?"

Leroy glanced at Matt, making a face like he couldn't believe anyone could be so stupid. "What do I care? Beer's beer. Just make sure you get real beer."

She frowned as she got to her feet. "What do you mean 'real' beer?"

"What the fuck you think I mean? Get beer, not cider or some goddamn flavored malt shit." He shook his head and looked at Matt again. "Go with her, man. Make sure she gets the right stuff."

Matt nodded and then he and the girl left the trailer together.

Leroy favored Chip with a big, shameless meth mouth grin. "Well, shit, buddy. Here we are. Alone at last. How you think we should spend this time together?"

Chip kept his mouth shut.

There was nothing productive he could say here and it hurt too much to talk anyway.

Leroy, however, *did* have some thoughts on the subject.

32

The only way Chip could cope as the rest of it played out was to think of what was happening to him as not real. You could only hurt so much before a part of your psyche became detached from the physical reality of it all. The pain was still there and was still terrible and excruciating, but a piece of him was able to sort of float above it all and just observe. To this part of his mind, it was all like a cheap play, a gritty drama enacted in some shabby theater by a group of lowlifes for that extra dose of hard-hitting realism. And everything took place in just the one room, because there was no room in the production budget for additional sets. The name of this harrowing tale of violence and degradation—*The Torture and Death of Chip Taylor*.

The drama was one lurid scene of depravity after another, an unrelenting and unflinching examination of humanity's cruelest, darkest impulses. The earlier bits showing Chip's arrival at the trailer and his early, almost successful attempt to get free of the situation were just the setup for the main event, existing only as a flimsy excuse for a prolonged indulgence in voyeuristic sadism. It was the kind of thing some critics might call "torture porn", thinly-veiled pseudo-entertainment intended mainly to satisfy the twisted appetites of all the closet sickies in the audience.

In one scene, a redneck meth dealer sexually assaults our "hero" when he is left alone with him for a brief time. In another scene, two of his fingernails are pulled out with pliers by the fat girl who steered him into this trap in the first place with her lies. The guys hold him down while the girls laugh at his screams. But eventually the fingernail removal sends one of the lowlifes running to the kitchen to vomit into the sink. Somehow this act is more nausea-inducing than the savage and bloody golf club beating that preceded it. There are brief periods of respite between the major acts of cruelty. The hero's tormenters drink and indulge in various substances. They dance and laugh and have a great time. The soundtrack is an endless succession of grating hip hop. The big bass thump makes the trailer's walls audibly vibrate. Empty beer cans and bottles pile up everywhere. Hours and hours pass. The daylight visible through the windows fades. Friends of the lowlifes visit the trailer and take turns either knocking the hero around or humiliating him in some way. It's a party and he is the main source of entertainment. The trailer's interior turns hazy with cigarette smoke and the hero becomes lightheaded. He is barely able to keep his eyes open. Someone hits on the idea of keeping him awake by burning his flesh with cigarettes. It works.

For a while.

A point came where Chip's tormentors were unable to keep his eyes open regardless of what they did to him. That sense of woozy detachment stayed with him

68 Kill

into unconsciousness. If he'd been capable of anything like coherent thought before that slide into deep darkness, he likely would have figured these were the last waking moments of his life—and he probably would have been okay with that after enduring so much trauma.

But Chip did wake up again.

And when he did...

33

Opening his eyes had never been so painful, not even after the worst hangover of his life, and he'd had some pretty epic ones in his time. His whole body—or so it seemed—was covered in welts and bruises. Even the slightest movement made him gasp in pain. At first he could only squint. The world around him was one big blur filled with swatches of faded color and suggestions of things that might have been shapes. The hangover-like ache in his head was made worse by the hip hop music still playing at a loud volume. This alone was confirmation that he hadn't died yet. He didn't know how he felt about that. On the one hand, there was some level of reflexive relief at finding himself alive. The feeling withered, however, as his mind began to work at something approaching full-speed. With increased clarity came the bitter realization that he remained captive in his own personal slice of hell.

But something was different. It took him many moments to begin to perceive the nature of the change. He only realized what the difference was when the world around him at last began to come into sharper focus. Though the music was still thumping, the buzz of excited conversation from before was gone. In fact, he heard no voices at all beyond the recorded one torturing the stereo system's speakers.

Chip saw bodies on the floor. He saw Monica and Leroy curled up together. Monica had a hand wrapped loosely around the neck of an almost empty Southern Comfort bottle. His 9mm was hanging out of Leroy's hip pocket. They were so perfectly still Chip first thought they might be dead. But then he detected the faint throb of a pulse in Monica's throat. That made him happy. He didn't want her to be dead yet.

He winced and bit back a cry of pain as he lifted his head and craned his neck around to take in the entire scene. Once he had surveyed it all, he felt an urge to laugh. But the smile that tried to form on his swollen lips died before it could really take shape. There was an element of something almost funny in the scene greeting him after his return to full consciousness, but any inherent humor was blunted by the vivid memory of the things that had been done to him. They were all passed out. Monica, Leroy, Matt, the big-breasted blonde whose name he still didn't know, and a couple other redneck bottom feeders who'd come over for the party. It was a deep state of unconsciousness that bordered on comatose, at least from the looks of it. The impression caused him to briefly think of Liza in her hospital bed back in Nashville, but he pushed the thought away. There was no room in his head for anything other than escaping this hellish place, which was a real possibility again thanks to a huge oversight on the part of his overly-impaired tormentors—no one had ever taken the time to bind him to the chair..

He had a window here. Not a big one, most likely. Though they all looked down for the count, he couldn't take that for granted. As long as he remained here, there was a chance one of more of them would wake up and take steps to correct the oversight. The smart move would be to gingerly limp out of here, take the Pontiac, and drive away before any of them could come out of their alcohol-induced deep slumbers. But as he sat there a moment longer and allowed himself perfect awareness of all the different parts of his body that ached and throbbed, he knew doing the smart thing was yet again not part of the agenda.

Another few moments passed as he steeled himself for the ordeal to come. It was precious time he knew he couldn't afford to waste, but it was necessary. He couldn't just propel himself out of the chair without screaming in pain. The pain would come regardless, but he needed to be psyched up and ready to put a lid on any verbal expression of it. While he did this, he stared at Monica's slack features and marveled at how innocent she looked in sleep. She was so young. Barely more than a kid. But there was evil inside her. The appearance of innocence was an illusion. A mask. He yearned to expose the monster lurking beneath it.

Chip gritted his teeth and began to rise from the chair. The effort nearly came to an immediate premature end. His left leg wanted to give out, but he tensed his muscles and stiffened the swollen knee as best he could. The leg was shaking badly, but it stayed under him as he got fully to his feet. The first steps he took sent jolts of severe pain up the length of both legs. The shaking got worse and he almost toppled over a few times. The worst of it was when he bent over to pluck the gun from Leroy's pocket. It took the most concentrated exertion of willpower he'd ever managed not to unleash an operatic scream as he did this. Leroy shifted a little in his sleep, rolling away from Monica as the gun came free of his pocket. Chip pointed the gun at his face, waiting to see if the punk would wake up.

But he did not.

Chip sighed.

Good.

He wasn't ready to deal with Leroy yet.

Unfortunately, he had another pressing issue to contend with before he could do anything else. It meant temporarily putting on hold any thoughts of vengeance or escape. Dealing with it might significantly increase the risk in a situation already fraught with it, but he had no choice if he meant to remain here long enough to accomplish all the things he hoped to do.

He turned away from the slumbering rednecks and lurched into the kitchen. A bathroom toilet would be more suitable to his needs, but he didn't think he could make it all the way to the opposite end of the trailer without either tripping over one of the prone white trash kids or pissing his pants. His swollen bladder felt ready to explode. In those moments, the strain of it was worse than any of his other many pains. But this was one pain he could at least temporarily alleviate.

Standing at the kitchen counter, he set down the gun and pushed down the front of the sweatpants to pull out his cock and aim it at the sink. This time no amount of willpower was able to hold back his loud groan of relief. A powerful stream of urine spattered a pile of dirty dishes. Chip kept his head tilted toward the ceiling until it began to ebb a little, biting down on his bottom lip against the sharp pain the simple act of urination was causing. There were multiple things wrong inside him, things caused by the many brutal beatings he'd taken. When he finally looked at the weakening stream, he was unsurprised by the faint reddish hue he saw.

Shit. That can't be good.

He was shaking out the last few drops of piss when he heard a creaking sound in the corner of the kitchen. His head snapped in that direction and he grimaced when he saw the rear door beginning to swing open. As he grabbed the gun off the counter, he hoped like hell it wasn't that goddamn Xbox-loving kid coming back for another shot at playing *Halo* or whatever the hell it was kids played these days. He took a few lurching steps toward the door and raised the gun with both hands. Kid or not, whoever was coming through that door was about to die.

It wasn't the kid.

Amy Hayworth came fully into the kitchen before she realized who was blocking her way. She stopped in her tracks when she saw him, her mouth opening in obvious shock. Whether the shock was more from the gun pointed at her face or seeing Chip on his feet was hard to say. She still looked drunk. Her cheeks were a deep shade of red and her eyes were bloodshot. Her hair was a ratty mess. Chip had no idea what she'd been doing outside and didn't care. He was more concerned by his failure to note her absence after regaining consciousness. But this was a good lesson in staying focused and not letting his guard down. No matter how close he imagined he was to having the situation well in hand, there were still too many unpredictable variables in play. Things could still go wrong a million different ways. It was time to start getting down to business before one of those things became his undoing.

Amy's shock gave way to a dull-eyed look of recognition and fear. She took a stumbling backward step before tripping over her feet and falling hard on her ass. The noise her tumble caused was significant. It made the dishes in the sink rattle. She gaped up at Chip and shook her head in tearful, terror-stricken bewilderment. Chip shot her through the forehead. A spray of blood, brains, and bone fragments went flying through the open door behind her.

He turned away from her and staggered back across the kitchen to check on things in the living room. The report of the gun had been loud, but not loud enough to rouse the sleeping cretins. Chip guessed he had the pounding music to thank for that. If these fools could sleep through that garbage, they could sleep through anything. But there was no guarantee someone from one of the neighboring trailers wasn't on the line with 911 right now. That probably wasn't the case—no one had called in a noise complaint after untold hours of loud-ass music—but it was just one more reason to accelerate things.

Chip lurched back into the living room and positioned himself close to where Matt was curled up with the nameless blonde while also keeping Leroy and Monica in full view. He stared at Monica's slack features for a moment before giving Matt and the blonde his full attention. She still looked nothing like a monster. It bothered him more than he wanted to admit.

He aimed the gun at Matt's face and squeezed the trigger. The bullet punched through the bridge of his nose and this time the report of the gun was enough to shock the blonde out of her deep sleep. She screamed when she saw the wreck that had been made of her boyfriend's head. She screamed again when she looked up at Chip and saw the gun aimed in her direction. He shot her in the throat and spun toward Monica and Leroy. The abrupt move almost caused his battered left leg to fold beneath him, but he again managed to stay upright. The mind-bending pain that came as a result of the effort made him scream, but that was okay now. The time for stealth was gone and the time to kill without mercy was at hand.

Leroy sat up with a dazed, sleepy look on his face. He patted at his pocket, instinctively feeling for the gun. Chip waited for the son of a bitch to look at him and then he shot him through his wide-open mouth. Blood and brains spattered Monica as she came awake with a shriek. She looked up at Chip and tried to scramble away from him, but she was still a touch too fogged by booze and sleep. He caught up to her and cracked the butt of the gun across her face. And then he did it twice more, breaking her nose and snapping off a couple of her perfect teeth.

A party guest made a break for the door.

Chip shot her in the back. Blood splashed against the door an instant before she fell against it and slid dead to the floor. That left just one other party guest, a fat guy with a goatee who ran for the bedroom. Chip hopped across the floor and caught up to him just as he stepped through the door. The fat guy cried and pleaded for mercy. Chip put the gun to his head and pulled the trigger.

They were all dead now.

All but one, that is.

Chip came back out of the room and saw Monica crawling across the floor toward the kitchen. He came at her with unhurried strides, savoring the hopelessness of her situation in a way that would have repulsed him twenty-four hours earlier. But he was no longer the man he had been a day ago. The flesh was still living, but that man was as dead as Ken McKenzie.

Monica was a special case. She had to suffer more than the rest. He couldn't just put a bullet through her head and be done with it. He had to make a wreck of her, had to make her scream, and when he saw the discarded golf club on the floor, he knew just how to do it. The pain was nothing now when he bent to retrieve it. It was there and later it would matter, but right now it did not. All that mattered was Monica.

She squealed when he halted her progress toward the kitchen with a foot pressed into the small of her back. Her scream when he flipped her over made him laugh. He tossed the gun aside and took a practice swing at her head with the club, making her flinch. There was still plenty of his blood on the clubhead. Soon her blood would be there, too. It would be a fitting union, an unholy matrimony of gore.

The first swing of the club pulverized her nose. She screamed and tried to roll away from him, but he seized her and threw her down onto her back again. The next swing of the club pulped her lips and broke off more of those teeth. The one after that broke her jaw. Even in his weakened condition, Chip was far stronger than Monica Delacroix had ever been. The next swing collapsed an eye socket. Each strike of the clubhead against her flesh made him feel a little better and with each blow a bit more of her former prettiness disappeared. After she stopped moving—or even reacting at all—he shifted his grip on the club and swung it straight down at her head, over and over, obliterating any identifiable trace of the girl she'd been. Chip tossed the club aside and stood there panting as he stared down at her.

Monica Delacroix was dead.

He spat on her ruined face. "Fuck you."

Chip knew he couldn't revel in the moment. The vengeance part of this was over. Now it was time to recover what had been taken from him.

34

The search for his things didn't take long. He found most of it in the bedroom stashed under a queen-sized bed with a sagging mattress, the same bed upon which Monica had earned her secondary income as a trailer park whore. All her stuff was secondhand and in rough shape. Even the first-generation Xbox looked like it had come from a pawnshop. This evidence of the shabby state of Monica's existence pleased Chip. She'd lived a hard life and had never accomplished much of anything. There'd likely been very little joy in any of it. And now she was dead and any chance at anything better was gone forever.

Good.

After finally shutting off the irritating music, Chip took a few minutes to clean up as best he could and change back into his own clothes. Now, as he sat behind the wheel of the Pontiac outside the trailer, he checked his reflection in the rearview mirror one last time before hitting the road. He was no longer covered in blood, but he still looked terrible. There were numerous visible gashes, welts, and bruises. He looked like he'd been on the losing end of the most brutal heavyweight title fight in the history of boxing. But this was a problem only time could fix. And even after he healed, there would be scars. He would never again quite be the "pretty boy" he'd once been. But so what? What counted was that he was still alive, which was more than he could say for a whole lot of other people.

    The money was on the seat next to him. He'd dripped blood on some of the bills when he'd opened the envelope to check it. There hadn't been time for a full count—plus he hoped to avoid thoroughly staining the bills crimson—but a quick flip through it verified it was mostly all there. The heft of it seemed about the same. He had a hunch a bit of it was gone, spent by Monica or Leroy on who knew what, but the bulk of it was there. He had to count his blessings, really. He'd come out of all this with his life and most of the money. Minus a girlfriend and another girl who might have become a girlfriend, but, hey, you couldn't have everything.

    Things could be a lot worse.

    Chip put on his seatbelt.

    It was time to go.

    He put the key in the ignition and glanced at the rearview mirror again as he shifted gears and prepared to back away from the trailer. A glimpse of shadowy movement caught his attention and he craned his neck around to stare at the trailer behind him. The movement he'd glimpsed had come from the far side of the trailer. It was still dark, but the glow of his taillights allowed him to make out the shape of the red Hyundai, which was still where he'd abandoned it earlier. Another car was parked next to it now. Someone with a flashlight was peeking inside the Hyundai.

    A lump lodged in Chip's throat.

The other car was a police cruiser and the person with the flashlight was a cop.

And now the cop was talking into a radio. Chip didn't need to hear his voice to know he was reporting the discovery of a murder victim's stolen car. For one blindingly terror-stricken moment, Chip almost allowed panic to paralyze him. But then he smiled and let out a breath. This moment of near-panic was only an echo of his former self. He had been tested in battle and had bathed in the cleansing blood of his enemies. He was someone else now. A different, stronger, better person. A person with no fear at all.

Chip let his foot off the Pontiac's brake pedal and backed away from Monica's trailer. He changed gears in an unhurried way and drove out of the trailer park at the sedate pace appropriate to a residential setting. Not once on the way out did he glance again in the direction of the cop and the stolen Hyundai. Shortly after he got out on the main road, a cop cruiser with its lights on went zipping by on its way to the trailer park. Yet another cruiser was close behind it. Unfazed, Chip continued toward the interstate junction at a hair over the speed limit.

At the junction, he took the westbound exit.

He didn't know where he was going.

Or who he would be when he got there.

Someone new, though, that was for sure. Someone unburdened with baggage or angst, an optimistic guy with some money in his pocket and much brighter prospects than before. The guy who had once been Chip Taylor turned on the radio and spun the dial until he found an oldies station. He cranked the volume and sang along with the Rolling Stones doing "Satisfaction" as he hit the interstate.

He had a moment of vaguely troublesome light-headedness some ten miles down the line. His eyes closed and the car swerved over the yellow line, but his eyes snapped back open and he was able to course-correct almost immediately. The troubled feeling departed as his newfound optimism reasserted itself. He was just tired. He'd been through a lot. The darkness was fading and the sun was rising. It'd all gone on a lot longer than he'd thought. He would stop somewhere and rest once he'd put some serious distance between himself and all that wreckage from his former life. His eyes fluttered and almost closed again for a very brief moment. He shook his head to clear the cobwebs and it seemed to work. Maybe he'd stop for a quick cup of convenience store coffee another ten or twenty miles down the road.

Yeah, that would probably be the smart thing to do.

A glance at the envelope of money further cemented his good mood.

He smiled.

His days of worrying about things were almost over.

THE END

ABOUT THE AUTHOR: Bryan Smith is the author of numerous previous novels and novellas, including The Killing Kind, House of Blood, Depraved, The Freakshow, Soultaker, Deathbringer, The Dark Ones, Kayla and the Devil, Kayla Undead, and The Diabolical Conspiracy. Most of these were first available via mass market paperback from Dorchester Publishing. Some have since been reprinted by Deadite Press. All are now available in Kindle editions. A new novel, The Late Night Horror Show, was released by Samhain Publishing in March of 2013. A second novel from Samhain, Go Kill Crazy!, is slated for February 2014. Bryan lives in Tennessee with a wide array of pets. Visit his home on the web at www.bryansmith.info.

Made in the USA
Coppell, TX
26 January 2021